DENNIS PIERCE

SWINGING FOR POWER

A Parker Hanson Mystery

First published by Hawkshaw Press 2024

This novel is entirely a work of fiction. The names, characters and incidents portrayed in it are the work of the author's imagination. Any resemblance to actual persons, living or dead, events or localities is entirely coincidental.

First edition

ISBN: 9798991643924

This book was professionally typeset on Reedsy.
Find out more at reedsy.com

"They laugh 'cause they know they're untouchable / Not because what I said was wrong."

—Sinead O'Connor, "The Emperor's New Clothes"

Acknowledgments

All of the events and characters portrayed in this story are fictitious. However, many of the novel's settings are real, as is much of the information behind the story—including the facts and figures about New Hampshire's forest lands.

Like investigating a criminal conspiracy, writing a novel takes an entire village, and I'm very grateful to many people for their assistance.

I'd like to thank Fire Chief Steve Sherman of the New Hampshire Forest Protection Bureau and Regional Forester Maggie Machinist of the New Hampshire Division of Forests and Lands for their time and insight into the state's forestry practices, as well as Public Information Officer Shelly Angers for connecting me. The Division of Forests and Lands really does create a "New Hampshire Forest Action Plan" every ten years, and the 2020 version was instrumental in my research.

A warm thank you to retired police Sergeant Austin Cote and Lieutenant Christopher Peach, retired Deputy Chief for the Nashua PD, for their insight into police procedures and chains of command. I'm sure I took many liberties with these procedures in the interest of creating a compelling story; to the extent that I have, this responsibility lies solely with me.

Librarians make the world go round, and I've never met a librarian who wasn't eager to help. I'm especially grateful to Reference Desk Librarian Marilyn Day and Reference

Archivist Jessica Holden at UMass Boston's Joseph P. Healey Library for their help in researching the university's history. I have also relied on Michael Feldberg's excellent book, *UMass Boston at 50: A Fiftieth Anniversary History of the University of Massachusetts Boston*, for my research.

Thank you to former U.S. Army Captain Tom LaBelle for sharing his Army Ranger experience with me in great detail. Tom, your insight helped me bring Amalia's character to life on the page, and I'm so proud to call you my nephew.

Thanks also to Realtor Marie Lamora for her real estate wisdom, which was pivotal in helping me think of having Parker pose as an appraiser. And though I wasn't able to connect with the sources they suggested, thanks to Yellowstone Ecological Research Center Advisory Board member Andy Lamora and Kelly Bell of the accounting firm Fraticelli & Company for their help in my research as well.

The character of Conrad Bellows was inspired by my own professional mentor, Gregg W. Downey, under whom I had the pleasure to work for many years. Gregg taught me everything I know about being an effective journalist, and he was the person who actually came up with the phrase "reporters, not repeaters." I'm so thankful for his guidance, and this book is dedicated to his memory.

Finally, I'd like to thank my entire family, without whom none of this would have been possible. I'm especially grateful for my dad, Dennis Sr., and his knowledge of classic cars—as well as my wife Jean and her never-ending support. I love you all so much.

Chapter 1

I n hindsight, it was a good thing the Red Sox blew a three-run lead against the Dodgers in the bottom of the ninth inning in Los Angeles.

Otherwise, I wouldn't have been awake to hear those two hitmen trying to break into my apartment.

Of course, I wasn't thinking that at the time. When the Sox closer gave up a three-run bomb to Dodgers superstar Mookie Betts, tying the game and sending the home crowd into a state of delirium, I let loose with a few choice bombs of my own.

Normally, I might have just gone to bed at that point. But my mind was still buzzing from what I'd learned for my client, Brooke Bowman, earlier that day. I knew I wouldn't be able to sleep, even though it was already one a.m., Eastern time. So I kept watching as the game went into extra innings.

My loyalty was rewarded when the Sox eked out a run in the top of the thirteenth and held on to win, 6-5. By that time, it was nearly three in the morning. I turned off the TV, groped my way to my bedroom in the dark, and collapsed into bed.

Not more than ten minutes later, I heard what sounded like faint scratching noises coming from outside the door to my apartment. I bolted upright and strained to hear in the dark.

There it was again, along with a low murmur of voices.

Someone was trying to pick the lock.

For any other private investigator, the prospect of a few thugs outside the front door in the middle of the night might provoke genuine excitement, a chance to prove one's valor.

That wasn't the case for me.

I'm not an ex-cop, or a veteran of the armed forces. Hell, I don't even own a gun. I'm a former investigative reporter who found himself out of a job when the newspaper business collapsed from the competition of free online content posing as "news."

My experience consisted of writing long-form stories about corruption, not strong-arming the wise guys responsible for it.

When I lost my reporting job, I figured I could put my investigative skills to good use as a private detective, tracking down long-lost acquaintances and maybe catching cheating spouses in the act. At worst, I thought I might have to deal with a few angry husbands—or wives—who wanted to extract payback for exposing their secrets. But I never imagined I'd be in any real danger.

What was I gonna do, hit those crooks outside my door with a well-placed metaphor?

My skill lay in telling a story. So that's what I set out to do.

I slipped out of bed and tiptoed to my bedroom window, which led to a back fire escape. I opened the window, whispering a silent prayer that my assailants weren't smart enough to position someone at the rear of the building. Then I hid inside the closet and waited, armed only with a baseball bat.

I was hoping they'd see the open window and jump to the wrong conclusion.

I had two other fervent hopes as well. One was that the pounding of my heart wouldn't give away my position. I had just undergone triple bypass surgery six months earlier. Now, it seemed as if my rebuilt heart was actually beating stronger—and *louder*—than it ever had before.

With apologies to Poe, I was worried that my own self-betrayal would be fueled not by guilt, but by the miracles of modern medicine.

My other concern was my choice of weapon. I had no doubt that I'd be vastly out-armed if my hiding place should be discovered. But what really bothered me was that I might actually have to *use* the bat. It was an autographed keepsake from Red Sox legend David Ortiz, and I'd hate to see it broken over some numbskull's skull.

Through a crack in the doorway, I watched as two men crept into the room. One had a handgun equipped with what looked like a silencer. When they saw the bed was empty, they turned and noticed the open window, its curtains gently flapping in the breeze.

Just as I'd intended, the gunman rushed to the window and pivoted out onto the fire escape, thinking he was hot on my trail, while his partner went out the front door of my apartment. I followed him and watched as he charged down the stairs and out of the building. Then I let out a deep breath, went back inside, and called the police.

Within ten minutes, I was talking with a dour-faced detective with blotchy skin while his partner perused my apartment for signs of the intruders.

"Did you get a look at the assailants?"

"No. They were both wearing ski masks."

"What about the gun? Did you happen to notice what kind

of handgun it was?"

"I have no idea. A big one. I'm not much of a firearms enthusiast."

The detective, who'd introduced himself as McDougal, failed to suppress a scowl.

"You've not been very helpful, Mr. Hanson."

After the police left my apartment, I tossed some clothes into a duffle bag and hightailed it to my car, a 1974 Dodge Dart parked a few blocks away. I drove from my apartment in a converted paper mill in downtown Manchester, New Hampshire, to the Manchester airport. It was just after four a.m., and there were very few other vehicles on the road. I had no trouble making sure I wasn't followed.

I stashed my car in the long-term parking section and secured a nondescript Ford Fusion from the rental counter. Then I drove back to the Holiday Inn on Brown Avenue. I checked into a room facing the rear of the building and dropped my bag on the bed.

But my adrenaline was still pumping, and I knew I wouldn't be able to sleep.

Instead, I walked next door to an all-night diner. Reluctantly passing up what used to be my go-to breakfast order—steak and eggs—I asked for decaf coffee (black) and an egg white omelet with spinach and tomatoes.

While I waited for the food to arrive, I thought about what the hell I was going to do next.

* * *

The trouble began earlier that week, when I met Ms. Bowman at a Starbucks on Route 28. Unlike the detectives in so many crime fiction stories, I don't maintain an office. As much as I love the Spenser novels, I never understood how Spenser could afford office space in downtown Boston, where the rent alone is a felony.

Anyway, I was sipping an unsweetened iced tea—and trying not to think about how I *really* wanted a white chocolate mocha latte—when Ms. Bowman walked in. "Look for a guy in his mid-forties with fair hair and glasses, wearing an olive green corduroy blazer," I'd told her.

She spotted me right away. "Parker Hanson?" she asked. I nodded and gestured toward the chair across from me.

Brooke Bowman was a striking woman in her mid-thirties, with long dark hair and an air of quiet sincerity. I liked her immediately. She proved to be well read also. When I told her I'd been a newspaper reporter before becoming a detective, she said, "Like Irwin Fletcher."

"No, nothing like Fletch," I corrected her. "He was a Lakers fan."

She told me her husband, Mark, worked as deputy chief of staff in the governor's office.

"Lately, Mark has seemed very distant, like he's keeping something from me," she confessed. "I think he might be having an affair."

If he is, then he's an idiot, I thought.

Out loud, I said: "What would you like me to do?"

"Find out what's going on. He won't talk to me about any of this. If he's in some kind of trouble, I want to help him. And if he's sleeping around, I want to know."

* * *

The morning after I met Brooke Bowman, I followed her husband from their home in Webster to the New Hampshire State House building in Concord, where Mark had an office. I parked on a side street where I could keep an eye on both the front and side entrances of the building. I wanted to see where he might go during the day.

Being an investigator requires a lot of watching and waiting for something to happen. Much of that idle time is spent waiting in a parked car. I've never been too keen on my first name; supposedly, my mother had a huge crush on Parker Stevenson from the old *Hardy Boys/Nancy Drew Mysteries* TV series in the late 1970s, and that was the source of her inspiration.

But as an investigator's name, Parker does have a certain logic to it.

Sitting in one place for hours at a time isn't so good for your health, though, especially when you're trying to stay alert. It typically requires a generous amount of caffeine, which—along with a poor family history—no doubt contributed to why I'd had a heart attack shortly before my forty-fifth birthday.

Since my surgery, I've been trying to eat healthier. I was popping clementine slices into my mouth when I spied Mark Bowman exit the State House through the side entrance shortly before noon. He looked around to make sure he wasn't being watched, then ducked into the passenger seat of a silver Volvo parked at the curb.

As the car pulled out into traffic, I caught a quick glimpse of the driver. She was an attractive woman with short brown hair, and she was smartly dressed. I put my own car in gear and fell in a few car lengths behind them, shielded from their view by a white box truck that had also just pulled into traffic.

The way Bowman had looked around, it was clear he didn't want to be seen. A clandestine meeting with an attractive woman in the middle of the day... It sure looked like Ms. Bowman's suspicion was correct.

I was going to have to break it to her that her husband was a giant ass.

Although I didn't miss churning out fifteen hundred words of copy on a tight deadline, there were many times I wished I was still behind the desk in my old newspaper office.

This was one of them.

The Volvo turned south on Main Street, followed by the box truck and me. A few blocks later, the Volvo turned right onto Route 202 and I kept pace. I knew the old Centennial Hotel was just up the road.

Was that where they were headed? I wondered.

I heard the collision almost before I saw it.

A giant dump truck, speeding down a side street from the right, barreled straight into the passenger's side of the Volvo, crushing it like a soda can.

The screech of metal scraping against metal tore the air.

Tiny glass fragments from the shattered windows of the car seemed to hang for a moment as if suspended, reflecting the rays of the early June sunshine, before pelting the hood of the dump truck like ice crystals in a hailstorm.

Gasping, I swerved to the side of the road and slammed my car into park. I leaped out and ran to the Volvo, which was already in flames. Clutching the driver's side door handle, I pulled as hard as I could. But the car was badly mangled, and the door wouldn't budge. Thick, acrid smoke filled my lungs and a searing wave of heat blistered my face, forcing me back from the car as I choked for breath.

The Volvo was now completely engulfed by fire. I sat down on the curb in a state of shock, barely aware of the sound of approaching sirens.

It had all happened so fast.

One second we were driving, and then … and then suddenly two people were dead. My client's husband, and the woman he was meeting.

That would be devastating under any circumstances. But the fact that I recognized the driver as I approached the car was a real punch to the gut.

Her name was Maggie Malone, and she worked for the *Concord Herald*. My old newspaper.

A former colleague, and a top-notch reporter.

As an ex-journalist, I take pride in my ability to find just the right words to describe any situation.

But at that moment, all I could think of was a single, wholly insufficient syllable.

Shit.

Chapter 2

I spent the next half-hour talking to a crash investigator while an EMT attended to my injuries. I had second-degree burns on my forehead, and my right eyebrow was singed. Plus, I'd inhaled a good amount of smoke into my lungs.

In speaking with the investigator, I learned that the driver of the dump truck had disappeared after the accident. The truck itself was reported stolen by a local construction company.

When I was given permission to leave, I drove back to my apartment in a daze. I was thinking of Brooke Bowman and what she must have gone through while I was being questioned.

The chiming of the doorbell, disrupting her life in a way that no one could truly prepare for.

The sight of the uniformed officers looking somber on her front steps, and the feeling of dread that something was terribly wrong.

The numbness she must have felt as she listened to the officers' words. The rise and fall of their voices, sounding as if they were coming from far away—like she was watching the scene unfold from outside her body.

And afterwards, once the officers had departed and the finality of the situation had begun to sink in, nothing but silence and emptiness and pain.

Not only had her world just been shattered, but she would be left with lingering uncertainty about the question she'd hired me to answer. Doubts about her husband's commitment to their marriage would echo long after he was gone, misgivings that the circumstances of his death only served to amplify.

And yet...

The fact that Bowman was meeting with Maggie cast the situation in a new light. In his position as deputy chief of staff for the governor, it wouldn't have been strange for him to be seen with the reporter who covered the political beat for the *Herald*.

And yet...

If the meeting really was innocent, then why was Bowman acting so suspiciously? Why did he glance around like he was worried about being seen?

Was it an affair, or something else?

Personal or professional?

I felt like I owed it to Ms. Bowman to find out. If I could answer that question for her definitively—better yet, if I could find some proof that her husband *wasn't* having an affair—then maybe she could make peace with his untimely death.

* * *

When I got home, I showered and changed clothes. Then I headed back up to Concord to talk with my former boss and mentor at the *Herald*, Conrad Bellows.

The newspaper's offices were located in a long, low-lying building on the Merrimack River. Inside, the newsroom looked like the image you see in the movies, with a lot of desks scattered around a wide-open bullpen—except only a few of the desks were being used, and the scene wasn't nearly as chaotic.

In fact, other than the muted clicking of computer keys from the handful of reporters who were there in the middle of the afternoon, the place seemed like a mausoleum.

Partly, that was a result of Maggie's death, which looked like it had cast a pall over the entire news team. But it also had to do with all the cutbacks the newspaper had been forced to make in recent years.

The newsroom looked a lot different when I started working there around the turn of the millennium.

Back then, when people still began their day by sitting down with their morning coffee and the newspaper, every desk in the newsroom was occupied. The collective energy in the room could have fueled the whole city as reporters worked the phones, discussed tactics with each other, dashed out to follow up on leads, and pounded out stories on deadline. Often, it was hard to hear yourself think amid the din.

That was before the Internet kneecapped the newspaper business.

When websites like Craigslist, eBay, and Facebook emerged, people no longer had to pay to take out classified ads in their local paper—and a key revenue source disappeared. Subscriptions also dried up as readers began turning to free content aggregation sites and social media platforms for their information. Page views quickly became the currency of the web, and suddenly anyone could post content and call it "news."

While some independent bloggers and content sites are doing terrific work in exposing injustice and pursuing the truth, there's also a lot of online junk masquerading as news.

Legitimate news organizations are competing for readers' eyeballs along with sites peddling conspiracy theories, rumors, and innuendo—and it's getting harder to distinguish between the real news sites and the pretenders.

With news, as with most things in life, you get what you pay for.

Conrad Bellows was part of the old guard of journalism. A newspaperman from another generation, he learned the trade back when the three-martini lunch was common. Now in his seventies, he could have retired from his job as editor-in-chief years ago. But that would have left a gaping hole in his life. Bellows saw reporting the news as a higher calling, and he believed he was playing a critical role in preserving our democracy.

When I first started working at the paper fresh out of college, I wrote a story about how researchers from the University of New Hampshire claimed to have discovered a nonfat substitute that tasted exactly the same as chocolate. Bellows summoned me to his office, shut the door, and proceeded to teach me a valuable lesson that has stayed with me ever since.

"We're *reporters*, not repeaters," he said. "If I wanted to know what the researchers alleged, I would have read the damned press release. Your job isn't to parrot what others tell you. It's to find out the truth."

A few months before I was "let go" amid a swath of cutbacks (a euphemism that never would have made it into a story edited by Bellows), the publisher held a meeting to announce that he'd hired someone to fill a brand-new position: director of online content. Besides pulling together our best stories and repackaging them for the web, this employee was also responsible for creating lighter, online-only content designed to increase page views for the newspaper's website, such as "top ten" lists and other clickbait.

True to his name, Bellows stood up in the middle of the meeting and roared, "What are we trying to be, the *Washington Post* or the Huffington Post?"

The door to Bellows' office was open as I approached. Inside, he was slumped at his desk, looking older and frailer than I remembered.

I knocked lightly on the door and poked my head into his office. "Hiya, chief."

He looked up, and a wan smile flashed across his face. "Hanson, how the hell are you?"

"Been better. We all have, I guess. I'm sorry about Maggie."

"Yeah." He took a bottle of twelve-year-old Macallan single malt scotch from the bottom drawer of his desk, poured himself a shot, and held the bottle out to me. Reluctantly, I passed. "Looks like we've got our front page story for tomorrow."

"You wouldn't happen to know why she was meeting with this Bowman guy, would you?"

He sighed. "No. She played things close to the vest."

"Any idea what stories she might have been working on?"

"She was following whether the state Legislature would vote on a bill to relax environmental regulations on manufacturers before the end of this year's session. She mentioned that she might have a lead on something pretty big as well, but there were a lot of loose ends she had to follow up on first."

"You don't have any other information on what this 'big story' was?"

"No. Too early for details."

"Okay, thanks. Sorry if I'm out of bounds here, but do you

happen to know if she was seeing anyone romantically?"

"You knew Maggie. She never really talked about her personal life."

"Got it. I'll be going now." I started to leave, but paused and turned back around. "You lost one of the good ones today."

He looked like a parent might look when you single out one of their children with praise. "They're all good."

On the way out, I took a circuitous route through the bullpen that brought me past Maggie's workspace. Her appointment book lay open on top of her desk. I slipped it under my jacket as I walked by.

I didn't think anyone would miss it.

***

Seated in my car, I opened Maggie's appointment book and glanced through the last few pages.

It showed that morning's rendezvous was at least her third meeting with Bowman in the last two weeks, a fact that wasn't suggestive either way.

There wasn't much else of interest in the book. She had been scheduled to meet with someone from an outfit called Tree Kings at four o'clock that afternoon. At first I thought it must have been a misspelling. But a quick Google search on my phone revealed that Tree Kings was a private forest management company based in Concord.

Clever name. But I didn't see any obvious connection with Bowman.

I started my car, changed the radio station to '80s pop music, and considered what I should do next.

I could drop in on Maggie's roommate to see if she might

know anything more about whom Maggie was seeing. Or, I could keep Maggie's four p.m. appointment with the forestry company, fumbling my way in the dark while trying to assess whether there was some sort of link to Bowman.

As Paul Reynolds, the lead guitarist for Flock of Seagulls, launched into his solo before the last verse of the band's hit song "I Ran"—and I marveled yet again that he was only nineteen when the song was released—I decided that Maggie's roommate seemed like the more attractive option.

I'd met her once before at a gathering at Maggie's apartment. Her name was Callie Stewart, and she was a dance instructor who worked evenings. She might have left for work already, but I was betting she would be taking the night off after hearing the news of Maggie's death.

I bet correctly. She answered the doorbell on my third attempt, dressed in a long gray sweater and black leggings. Her eyes looked puffy, as if she had been crying.

"Hi Callie, I'm sorry to bother you. I know this is a bad time, but I was a friend of Maggie's. I'm also a private investigator, and I have some questions about what happened today."

"I remember you from the party a few years ago." She stepped back so I could enter the apartment.

I followed her to the living room, where she offered me a seat in a navy-blue barrel chair while she took the couch.

"Would you like something to drink? We have water, lemonade, white wine." She realized her mistake in saying "we," and her face turned the color of oatmeal.

"I'm really sorry. We can do this another time if you'd like." I got up to leave.

"No, please stay. I … it's just that this place seems so quiet without her."

I sat back down. "I know this is a personal question, but was Maggie dating anyone in particular?"

"She went out with different guys from time to time, but there was nobody special. Like, she didn't have a boyfriend or anything."

"Do you happen to know any of their names?"

"There was a guy named Chad, a musician who plays in some local clubs. And someone else named Scott. I think he worked in finance."

"When Maggie was killed, she was driving with this man here." I showed her a picture. "His name is Mark Bowman. Have you seen him before?"

"No."

"Did Maggie ever mention him to you? Any idea what she might have been doing with him this morning?"

She shook her head.

I wasn't getting anywhere, and I felt like I was intruding on her grief. "Thank you, Callie," I said, rising to leave again. "I really appreciate your time."

She followed me to the door, looking like she was holding herself together with duct tape and baling wire.

"You know, when I worked with Maggie at the *Herald*, the news team had a weekly contest to see who could come up with the best pun," I told her. "The winner didn't have to chip in for Friday's lunch. Maggie won that contest more often than the rest of us combined. There was this one time when the reporter who compiled the local crime section was talking about a guy who drove off the road and into someone's living room. Apparently, this guy told the cops he hadn't slept for like forty-eight hours. Without missing a beat, Maggie says, 'So what did they book him for, resisting *a rest*?'"

That drew a smile.

"I was there when the accident happened," I added quietly. "I tried to get Maggie out of the car, but I couldn't. The fire spread too quickly. For what it's worth, I don't think she suffered. I think she was unconscious the whole time."

"Is that how you got hurt?" Callie said, indicating the bandage on my forehead.

"Yeah." I handed her my card. "If you have any information about that guy I showed you—or if you need anything at all—give me a call."

* * *

I didn't feel like contending with the rush hour traffic on Route 93, so I took South Street out of Concord and drove home to Manchester along back roads. On the way, I stopped at a local farm stand in Dunbarton and picked up some fresh early-season vegetables to make a salad for dinner.

After my heart surgery, I'd learned that eating healthy wasn't all that bad, but you had to plan ahead. That was the hardest part. When you're tired after a long day, or you don't have much food in the refrigerator, it's easy to fall back on takeout.

If you really want a shock, start paying attention to how much sodium there is in the average meal from a restaurant.

On the way up to my apartment, I ran into my downstairs neighbor, Amalia Velasquez. A bartender at a local establishment called the Tipsy Moose, she's also one of the few women to have completed the brutal Army Ranger School.

"Whoa, what happened to your face?" she asked.

"Plastic surgery gone horribly wrong."

"Who's your doctor, Frankenstein?"

"Good one. Have a nice evening."

"Hey, I have tonight off from work. Kris is coming over and we're going to watch a movie. Want to join us?"

"Thanks. That's kind of you to offer. But I don't want to be a third wheel." Kris was Amalia's girlfriend. "Besides, it's been quite a day. All I want to do now is crash."

"Okay. Catch you later."

Quite a day. That was an understatement.

Chapter 3

I didn't get much sleep that night. The image of the burning Volvo kept flashing into my head.

At five-thirty a.m., I gave up on trying to sleep and got out of bed. I walked down to the Merrimack River and followed a portion of the Heritage Trail, then returned home and ate a light breakfast of smoked salmon on toasted ciabatta bread and freshly squeezed orange juice.

After breakfast, I drove across the river to Catholic Medical Center for a round of cardiac rehab.

For heart patients who've never been active before, cardiac rehab is a good introduction to the world of exercise. For those who were active before experiencing heart problems, it's a way to ease back into exercising safely.

Considering that I ran three miles a day before my heart attack, pedaling for thirty minutes on a stationary bike while keeping my heart rate under the target for my age, 130 beats per minute, seemed pretty easy.

But I didn't mind. In fact, I looked forward to these appointments as an opportunity to regain some normalcy after being immobilized for three months following my surgery.

There were four of us in the class, which met three times per week.

There was Burt, a former chiropractor (now retired), who owned a winter home in Sarasota, Florida.

There was Joe, a former accountant (now retired), who owned a winter home in Bradenton, Florida.

There was Mickey, a former electronics salesman (now retired), who spent his winters in Fort Myers, Florida.

And there was me.

I was the only one in the class under the age of sixty-five.

You might think that would be awkward. But the truth was, I enjoyed our thrice-weekly banter, which mostly consisted of the same few topics. Sports, of course. Cars. How much we missed the foods we were no longer allowed to eat. And busting on each other.

"What the hell happened to your face?" said Joe as I entered the room. "It's actually an improvement."

"What'd you do, pick a fight with a rabid gerbil?" Mickey piled on.

"Yeah, but you should see the gerbil," I replied, attaching the leads of a heart rate monitor to my chest.

"Speaking of fights, how about the Sox last night?" Burt asked.

"It's about time they showed some fight," Joe said. "These players today, they could never cut it playing with the likes of Yaz and Fisk."

"Okay, everybody grab a dumbbell and let's get started," said Patty, the nurse who ran the program.

"That's what Joe's wife is thinking to herself whenever they go to bed," Mickey quipped.

* * *

After my rehab session, I went home and took a long, hot shower, then put a fresh bandage on my forehead.

Showered, dressed, and feeling much better after working up a light sweat, I decided to go on a fishing expedition.

I printed Maggie's photo from the staff section of the *Herald* website. Then I drove back to Concord with the photos of Maggie and Mark in hand. I figured I would spend the day showing them around at hotels and restaurants to see if anyone had seen the pair together. If so, I was hoping I could ascertain why.

I knew it was a long shot. But I didn't have much else to go on.

After a few hours I had only gotten one bite, and it was too small to keep. It turned out that a waitress at the Granite, the restaurant at the Centennial Hotel, had served them both late afternoon drinks a few days before. They requested a table near the back and each had one round, but that was it. Their conversation was hushed, and the waitress had no idea what they talked about. What's more, they showed no obvious signs of physical intimacy while they were there.

It was nearly two p.m., and I was debating whether I should just cut bait and go home when my phone rang. It was Callie, and she sounded upset.

"I was out running errands this morning, and someone broke into my apartment while I was gone," she sobbed. "They must have been looking for something. Everything's a mess."

"Have you called the police?"

"Not yet. I had your card, and I thought of you. I figured it might have something to do with Maggie and those questions you were asking yesterday."

"Okay, listen carefully. Go to a neighbor's apartment and

wait for me to call. If none of your neighbors are home, you can wait in your car with the doors locked. I'll be there as soon as I can."

***

When I pulled up in front of Callie's apartment, I gave her a call, and she met me outside her front door.

Inside, the apartment was just as she described. Kitchen and bathroom cabinets stood ajar. The drawers from desks and dressers were lying open, their contents having been rifled through. Couch cushions and bedroom mattresses were overturned. Pictures hung askew on the walls.

I checked in every room to make sure the intruders were gone, then poured a glass of wine for Callie to calm her nerves.

"Have you checked to see if anything is missing?" I asked.

"Not yet."

"Why don't you do that now, while I call the police. But try not to touch anything until they get here."

***

Two detectives showed up to Callie's apartment about fifteen minutes after I'd called the police. I knew one of them from my time as an investigative reporter. His name was Frank Connor, and he was the only Black detective on the Concord police force.

A tall man in his mid-fifties, Connor was wearing a green-and-gold windbreaker emblazoned with the words "Bishop Brady High School Basketball" from back in his playing days. Whenever I saw him, he was always chewing on some kind of bite-sized candy. Today it was a piece of Bit-O-Honey that he produced from his pocket, twisted off the wrapper, and placed into his mouth.

I swear, he must have owned a penny candy store on the side.

"Hanson, I should have known you'd be mixed up in this," he greeted me as his partner began snapping photos.

"Nice to see you, too, Detective."

"Was anything stolen?"

"Nothing that I could tell," Callie replied.

"Any idea who might do this, or what they were looking for?"

"No, not really."

"Okay. We'll have a look around, take some prints."

The simple truth was, I didn't have any idea who'd tossed the apartment or what they were looking for. But I suspected it had something to do with Maggie, and possibly Bowman as well. That is, unless there was a rival dance company instructor on the loose in Concord with an ax to grind against Callie—or maybe someone looking for an extra pair of ballet slippers.

After Connor and his partner left, I helped Callie straighten the place up again.

"I feel so violated," she said as we worked. "I mean, they went through my underwear drawer."

"Do you have another place you can stay for a few days, just in case whoever did this comes back?" I asked her.

"I can stay with my sister and her husband in Derry, I guess."

"Good. Why don't you do that. I wouldn't want anything to happen to you."

She leaned forward and kissed me lightly on the cheek. "Thank you. You've been so nice."

* * *

As I left Callie's apartment, there were two thoughts competing for my attention. One was how good she had smelled when she kissed me. Her shampoo, soap, and perfume made an intoxicating blend that smelled like jasmine and lilac. But I tried to push that thought out of my head and focus on the case instead.

Whatever the intruders had been looking for in Maggie's and Callie's apartment might have something to do with Maggie's connection to Bowman, I surmised. But what, exactly, was the nature of their relationship?

Was it a jealous lover of Maggie's, looking for evidence of an affair with Bowman? Could it have been my client, Brooke? Or did Maggie's secretive meetings with Bowman have anything to do with that "big story" Bellows had alluded to? And if so, was that the reason her apartment had been searched?

If I could figure out what Maggie had been working on for the paper, then I might be closer to answering those questions.

Before driving away, I called the *Herald* offices and asked for Jason Whitney, the newspaper's IT director.

There was a folder stored on the *Herald*'s private network where reporters kept their notes and documents pertaining to stories they were working on. I wanted to know what happened to a reporter's digital archive when that employee left the newspaper or died.

"The managing editor goes through that person's files with someone from HR to determine whether there's anything useful to the paper," Whitney said, "like notes on a story in development or corroborating evidence for an article we've already published. Then, everything else is deleted."

"Has that process happened yet with Maggie's information?"

"No. We need an official death certificate first."

When I worked at the *Herald*, I had been friendly with Jason. We'd had a few beers after work, even played disc golf together once or twice. I knew that what I was about to ask would be taking advantage of a friendship. But you can't win if you don't play the hand. The worst thing that could happen was that he'd say no.

"I don't suppose you could let me see what's in Maggie's folder before it's deleted? It's important to a case I'm working on. Otherwise, I wouldn't ask."

Jason hesitated before responding.

"I shouldn't do this without a court order. But I know you won't abuse the information. I'll send you what I can tonight."

"Thanks. I owe you."

"You owe me *big time*."

***

I had another stop to make before driving home. It was something I'd been putting off since the previous day, but I couldn't postpone it any longer.

I swung by a florist's shop and picked out a sympathy bouquet. Then I headed over to the Bowman household to see my client.

The Bowmans lived in an estate off Route 127 in Webster, set back quite a distance from the road. The driveway passed a fenced-in paddock on the left, where two chestnut-colored horses were grazing in a pasture. It curled up to a sprawling yellow farmhouse with white trim and a wraparound porch. Beside the house was a matching yellow barn with a square white cupola topped with an antique bronze weathervane.

Brooke answered the door, looking like she hadn't slept since the accident. I handed her the flowers and said, "I'm so sorry for your loss."

"Come in," she said, stepping aside so I could enter.

"That's okay. I can't stay. I just wanted to offer my condolences and give you a quick update on that matter you hired me to look into."

She came out onto the porch and shut the door behind her. Even though the day was warm, she wrapped her arms around her body, as if she were cold.

"I'm assuming the police told you that Mark was in a car with another woman when he was killed?"

"They told me that, yes."

"The woman was a reporter for the *Herald*. Someone I used to work with. Mark could have just been a source."

"But you don't know for sure."

"No, I don't know for sure. But I'm working on it."

"Thank you. That won't be necessary. I'll send you a check for your services to date."

I paused, trying to find the right words to say. I didn't want to be indelicate. But I thought she was making a mistake.

"Ms. Bowman, don't you want to know the truth?"

"My husband is gone. What difference would it make now?"

"If it were me, I'd want to know."

She looked at me intently, as if sizing me up. Her eyes settled on the bandage on my forehead.

"The police said you'd tried to help. Is that how you were injured?"

"Yes. I'm sorry I couldn't do more."

"Sometimes there's nothing more you *can* do. Thank you

for the flowers, by the way. They're very nice."

With that, she turned around and headed back inside.

* * *

On my way home, I stopped at a local seafood market and bought a fresh swordfish steak. I topped the swordfish with some pepper, dill, and freshly squeezed lemon juice, then put it in the oven to broil. While the fish was broiling, I sautéed some asparagus with olive oil and freshly ground pepper. I also got out the rest of the salad left over from the previous night.

I sat down at the table with my dinner and my laptop, ready to catch up on email as I ate.

Along with the usual spam mail offers, there was a message from a friend of mine in the state court system, asking if I could serve a summons to a guy who was skipping out on his child support payments.

Since I was once again unemployed, I gladly accepted the offer.

As I was reading through the rest of my email, I received a message from Jason. It contained an attachment labeled "Maggie info."

Technically, Brooke Bowman was no longer my client. I suppose I should have just let the matter drop. But I've never been someone who knows when to quit.

I unzipped the attached file and opened the resulting folder.

Inside, there were a number of sub-folders. Most of them had no apparent connection to the case, but there was one titled "govfraud" that seemed like it might be relevant. The corresponding metadata showed that it was the folder Maggie had created most recently.

I opened the "govfraud" folder. It contained two audio files with the file name "MB" and a date. These dates matched up with the dates of Maggie's first two meetings with Bowman. There were also a dozen or so JPG image files.

I clicked on the first of the two audio files. After a few seconds of muffled background noise, I heard Maggie's voice chime in clearly: "Can you state your name and title for the record?"

"My name is Mark Bowman, and I'm the deputy chief of staff for New Hampshire Governor Jack Gordon."

Bingo.

Bowman was indeed a source for one of Maggie's stories, and here was proof. Brooke would be happy to learn this fact, even if she did terminate our contract.

The recording continued: "Mr. Bowman, you called me from your office in the New Hampshire State House a few days ago with a serious allegation. Could you repeat for the record what you told me that day on the phone?"

"Yes. I said I believed there might be widespread fraud within our state procurement process."

I paused the recording. *Holy crap.*

No wonder Maggie's apartment was ransacked. If someone in the governor's office knew she was pursuing this story, who knows what they would have done to prevent it from seeing the light of day.

This also explained why Bowman was acting so furtively when I saw him exit the State House, and probably around his wife as well.

There would be plenty of time to listen to the whole recording later. But first, I was curious to see what the image files contained. I opened a few of the files and discovered they were photos of documents taken with a camera phone.

One of the file names caught my eye. It was titled "TreeKings_bid." The same firm that Maggie was supposed to meet with on the day she was killed.

I clicked on the file to open it. It was a photo of a state contract proposal written on company stationery. When I noticed the company's logo at the top of the proposal, my insides froze.

It was an image of a gold crown with three points, but each of the points was a miniature fir tree.

I had seen that image before. Painted on the side of the box truck that had been following Maggie's car shortly before it was rammed.

Oh my God.

As a former reporter, I don't believe in coincidences. When seemingly disparate events are connected, there's usually a reason. It's a sign that a pattern is emerging, warranting further investigation.

At that moment, my instincts were telling me that maybe the crash that killed Maggie and Mark wasn't an accident after all.

Maybe it was murder.

Chapter 4

The sun streaming through my bedroom window the next morning woke me up well before I was ready to face the day.

I dragged myself out of bed, put on a pair of sweatpants, and made my way to the kitchen. I juiced an apple, three carrots, and two celery stalks. I drank the juice and also swallowed the morning assortment of pills I would be taking for the rest of my life. Then I grabbed my keys and headed out for a walk around the block while I thought about what I'd discovered the night before.

I had been up late poring over Maggie's notes and listening to her conversations with Bowman. I'd learned that Tree Kings had been awarded a state contract as part of an effort by the Gordon administration to privatize a number of public services, supposedly in order to streamline state government agencies and boost efficiency.

The contract called for Tree Kings to manage some two hundred thousand acres of state forest land under the oversight of the New Hampshire Division of Forests and Lands, a branch of the state Department of Natural and Cultural Resources.

The scope of the work included surveying the state's forests and maintaining their health using techniques such as timber harvesting, tree planting, controlled burning, and getting rid of invasive plant and insect species that threatened to damage New Hampshire's woodland ecosystems.

The contract included a commission on the sale of all timber removed to keep the state's forests healthy, plus a flat fee per acre that covered turnkey forest management services. However, a major business rival, Donovan Forestry Services, had grown suspicious when Tree Kings won this three-year state contract for the third time in a row by bidding just a fraction of a penny under what Donovan Forestry had bid per acre each time.

If something like that happens once, you might chalk it up to bad luck. Maybe even twice. But three consecutive bidding cycles? Something didn't smell right.

Lachlan Donovan, the owner of Donovan Forestry Services, filed a challenge with the state procurement office, as losing bidders are within their rights to do. But the challenge was quickly dismissed.

Donovan then filed a complaint with the state Department of Labor. Without any evidence of wrongdoing, this complaint, too, went nowhere.

Unable to shake the feeling that his company was being cheated, Donovan reached out to Bowman's office.

A governor's chief of staff is like the chief operating officer for the state executive branch. Chiefs of staff manage the governor's time and make sure state officials are focused on the governor's priorities. But they also manage the unexpected. They serve as chief strategist, policy advisor, and crisis coordinator all in one.

As deputy to Chief of Staff Bryce Kilcullen, one of Bowman's responsibilities was to make sure there wasn't a scandal that could derail the governor's agenda.

Bowman told Maggie that he took Donovan's call himself. His initial impression was that Donovan's allegation seemed thin and most likely stemmed from Donovan's frustration at being passed over repeatedly for a contract. However, because Bowman was thorough and took his job seriously, he had a friend from the state IT department take a closer look.

As it turned out, the IT employee found evidence that someone had tapped into the computer system that companies use to submit bids for state contracts and changed Tree Kings' bid *after* the submission deadline.

While this wasn't definitive proof of tampering or bid rigging, it was strongly suggestive that the fix was in. Yet, when Bowman brought this finding to his boss's attention, Kilcullen seemed unconcerned.

For its part, the state procurement office claimed there was a problem with the bidding system and noted that some of the bids had to be reentered manually after the deadline. While IT said they had no record of any problems with the system, they acknowledged it was possible the procurement office was telling the truth.

To everyone else in Gordon's administration, the issue was considered resolved. But Bowman, being a person of high integrity, wasn't content to let the matter rest.

Bowman had the distinct impression that multiple people within the state government wanted to bury Donovan's complaint and move on. But why? Were they directly involved in a criminal conspiracy? And if so, how far did it reach?

Unsure of whom he could trust, Bowman decided to enlist the help of the press.

Bowman had given Maggie digital copies of all the written

documentation that existed in the matter. After talking with Bowman, Maggie had interviewed the head of the procurement office and Kilcullen to corroborate the facts, but that was as far as she'd gotten with her own research.

Before she and Bowman had been killed.

* * *

I circled the block twice as I thought about what to do with this information. Then I went back to my apartment to shower.

The idea that Mark and Maggie might have been murdered for what they knew had me rattled. But I couldn't just go to the police with my suspicions.

For one thing, I didn't have any hard evidence to support my theory. All I had was a recollection and a strong gut feeling there was foul play involved.

I was as sure as I knew the words to "Sweet Caroline" that the box truck I'd seen pull into traffic behind Maggie and Mark just a few minutes before they were killed belonged to Tree Kings.

Knowing everything I knew now, I'd bet my Pedro Martinez autographed baseball from the seventeen-strikeout, one-hit game he threw against the Yankees in 1999 that the occupants of the box truck were in contact with the driver of the dump truck the whole time, describing the route that Maggie and Mark were taking so he'd know exactly where to ram them.

But if I mentioned that to the police without producing anything resembling proof, I would have been laughed out of the station house.

Plus, I couldn't reveal how I knew of the connection between Maggie's story and Tree Kings without betraying Jason's confidence. The last thing I wanted was for Jason to get into trouble for breaking the rules on my account.

I needed something more concrete before involving the cops. That meant digging around for myself first.

And probably tipping off the crooks who'd killed Maggie and Mark for doing the same thing.

Welcome to the big leagues, kid.

* * *

I spent the rest of the morning doing research on my laptop. The first thing I wanted to know was the scope of the potential fraud. If Donovan's company was indeed the victim of bid rigging, had this happened to other firms as well, perhaps in other areas of state contracting?

I used the Manchester City Library's NewsBank database to search for any news stories about alleged purchasing fraud within the state government going back at least five years.

My search came up empty.

I also combed through public state records for other examples of complaints from losing bidders. Remarkably, there were very few—and the ones that did exist seemed more like sour grapes than legitimate grievances. None of the losing bids were within a few dollars of the winners.

Just to be sure, I even looked up the losing bidders from a number of state contracts in the past year and called them to see if they suspected any fraud.

None did.

Was it possible the alleged bid rigging on behalf of Tree Kings was an isolated example?

I also tried to learn as much as I could about the company at the center of the case.

From its website, I found out that Tree Kings had been in business for nearly eight years, around the same length of time that Governor Jack Gordon had been in office. The company was based in Concord, and it also maintained an outpost in the town of Pittsburg, New Hampshire, in the very northern reaches of the state.

Expanding my search, I learned that Tree Kings was owned by a local entrepreneur named Kyle Hammond. It wasn't hard gathering information on Hammond, as he seemed to relish publicity. A profile in *New Hampshire Business Review* revealed that Hammond was a graduate of Dartmouth College and the University of Pennsylvania's Wharton School of Business. Besides the forestry company, he owned a car dealership and a local restaurant chain. He also liked to hunt.

A forest management firm seemed like an odd choice for an Ivy League business graduate to invest in. I wondered what had drawn him to that business in particular.

While I was on my laptop, I searched for information about the delinquent father I'd agreed to serve with a court summons.

His name was Travis Tanner. He was a 2007 graduate of Manchester Central High School, and his last known address was in Hooksett. I managed to find a few recent photos of Tanner online, but I couldn't find any employment information for him within the last decade.

After spending several hours on my computer, I needed a break.

I filled a flask with water and headed over to the Manchester Court House to pick up the summons. Then I drove out to Massabesic Lake, stopping at Moe Joe's on the way for a caprese sandwich on a toasted baguette.

I took the food to go, parked by the Rockingham Rail Trail, and found a bench where I could sit by the water. While I ate my sandwich, savoring every bite, I watched the tree swallows darting and diving near the water's surface.

My stomach full and my mind finally clear, I drove up to Hooksett to see if I could find Tanner.

* * *

The address I had for Travis Tanner was a 1950s style ranch house on a side street off Route 3. The paint was peeling and the shingles were covered with moss. A buckling concrete walkway led to the front steps.

I pressed the doorbell twice, then stood back and waited.

A burly man with close-cropped white hair and a drooping mustache opened the door. He wore a black tank top and cargo shorts. He squinted at me through the smoke coming from the cigarette dangling from his lips.

"Whaddaya want?"

"Does Travis Tanner live here?"

"Nope. Haven't seen him in months."

"How do you know him?"

"My son." There was a measure of disappointment in his voice.

"I don't suppose you'd know where I could find him?"

"He in trouble?"

"No," I lied.

"Try Scott's Shots. He hangs out there a lot." A bar up the road on Route 3.

"Would he be there now, you think? Or is he at work?"

"Work? I guess you don't know him very well." He paused

to spit on the front step. "If they're serving, there's a pretty good chance he's drinking."

* * *

Scott's Shots was located between a fireworks store and a tattoo parlor. The southern New Hampshire trifecta. All that was missing to complete the tableau was a firing range and a pawn shop.

As I walked inside from the bright sunshine, I paused, letting my eyes adjust to the dimness.

The place looked like a cheap knockoff of the Hooters franchise. There was seating around the perimeter of the room, cafe-style tables on one side and booths on the other. A large rectangular bar filled the center. Two cocktail waitresses stood in a corner, laughing about something. The waitresses were dressed in tight-fitting, low-cut tee shirts, Daisy Duke shorts, and cowboy boots.

The building was mostly empty at that mid-afternoon hour. I scanned the few occupants in the room but didn't see Tanner among them.

I sat at the bar and ordered a club soda, which the bartender placed in front of me without saying a word. I suppose a beer might have hidden my intentions more effectively, but only for another minute or so. I already blended in about as well as a Baptist on Bourbon Street. Once I started asking about Tanner, it would be pretty clear why I was there.

Instead of playing a role, I tried a different kind of subterfuge.

"Know a guy named Travis Tanner?" I asked the bartender. "I was told he hangs out here quite a bit."

"We get a lot of people in here," the bartender responded, wiping off glasses and putting them back in a rack above the bar. He'd still barely made eye contact with me since I'd walked in.

"Oh, I'm sure you do. It's just that … okay, I'm going to level with you." I leaned forward conspiratorially. "I'm a private investigator, and I was hired by a former classmate of his, Kim Bouchard. Apparently, she had a real crush on him back in the day. Now she's coming off a nasty divorce. Alone again after ten years of marriage, she got to thinking: Whatever became of that guy Travis she thought was so cute in high school?"

I showed him a picture of Ms. Bouchard that I'd printed from a social media website.

Kim was real, but the story was not. She was a classmate of Tanner's from Manchester Central whom I'd found online. I figured I'd need a good incentive to lure Tanner out of hiding.

With guys like that, it wasn't hard to come up with an enticement that would work.

The bartender looked at the photo with interest. I guess I'd done my job well.

"If you see Travis, please tell him I'm looking for him. But here's the thing: I'm kind of in a rush. Kim's sister is trying to convince her to move out to California with her next week. Kim thought she'd try a Hail Mary first, see if there might be a reason to stay."

Every good sales pitch needs a sense of urgency to get people to act.

"I'll be back here Saturday afternoon at four o'clock if he's interested. If he's not here, I'll assume he's not—and that's what I'll tell my client."

With that, I left the bar.

* * *

I had one more story to peddle that afternoon. When I got back to my car, I dialed the number for Tree Kings and asked for the person who handles press inquiries.

"Hello, Monica Wyman speaking."

"Monica? Hi. I'm a freelance reporter, and I'm working on a feature story for *New Hampshire Magazine* about some of the state's biggest entrepreneurs and the keys to their success. I was hoping I could speak with Kyle Hammond for my story."

I had a hunch that playing to Hammond's ego would be the right approach in getting him to talk. It turns out I was right.

"I'm sure Mr. Hammond would be happy to speak with you for your story. Let me just check on his availability, and I'll get back to you soon."

"Thanks, Monica. You're a big help. The problem is, my editor is really riding me to get him the story by early next week. Is there any chance I could talk with Mr. Hammond in the next few days?"

"Let me see… Mr. Hammond has some availability tomorrow afternoon. Would three o'clock work for you?"

"Three is perfect."

"Would this be a Zoom call?"

"Actually, I'm local. If it's not too much trouble, I'd love to meet with him in person. Maybe I could get a tour of the facility as well?"

"Yes, I'd be happy to set that up for you."

"Wonderful. Thanks so much for your help. I look forward to seeing you both tomorrow."

* * *

The call to Tree Kings completed, I went to a package store and bought a twelve pack of locally brewed IPA. I drove over to Jason's house in Concord and left the beer on his front porch, along with a note that said: "Thanks for your help!"

Then I drove up to Webster to see Brooke Bowman. I thought she should know what else I'd managed to learn since we last spoke—and what I suspected about her husband's death.

But as I drove up her driveway, I saw that she had company.

There were three other cars parked in front of her house. Relatives, maybe, in town for Mark's funeral that weekend.

I was glad she wasn't alone. But I didn't want to intrude, even though I was hoping to speak with her in person.

Instead, I wrote out a note asking her to call me and left it in her mailbox. Then I headed back home to Manchester.

When I got back to my apartment, it was after six in the evening. I put a pot of water on the stove to boil, and when the water was ready I added a half cup of quinoa. While the quinoa was cooking, I diced a red onion, a tomato, and an avocado. I mixed the vegetables together with the quinoa and some chickpeas in a bowl for a quick dinner. For flavor, I squeezed a fresh lime over the mixture.

I ate dinner at my laptop while I checked my email and caught up on the news of the day. Then I flopped down on the couch and turned on the TV. Because the Red Sox were off, I flipped through the channels looking for something else to watch.

I stopped when I came upon a broadcast of *Casablanca*. Although I'd seen the movie so many times I could quote much of the dialog in sync with the actors, I could never pass it up whenever I saw it was on.

My lack of sleep since witnessing Mark's and Maggie's murder caught up to me, though. As Mr. and Mrs. Leuchtag, the German couple at Rick's Cafe who are trying to learn English before immigrating to America, might say, I didn't make it past "eight watch" before falling asleep soundly on the couch.

Schlaf gut.

Chapter 5

Without any outside stimulus to wake me, I might have slept until noon the next day. However, I'd set the alarm on my phone so that I wouldn't miss my next cardiac rehab session. I was looking forward to tackling the stationary bike and working off some of the tension from the last few days.

I punished the stationary bike until my quads hurt, keeping my heart rate around the upper threshold of what I was permitted nearly the whole time. By the time I was done, my entire body was dripping with sweat.

As I left the hospital, I saw that Brooke had called and left a message during the rehab session. I called her back, and we agreed to meet at the Starbucks on Route 28 again later that morning.

When Brooke walked in, I was sipping an orange-flavored San Pellegrino and trying to avoid eye contact with the assortment of sugary pastries behind the counter. Although she seemed tired and less animated than in our first meeting, which wasn't at all surprising, she looked like she was coping okay with her loss.

"I'm sorry to take up your time when you have so much going on, but I have some important information about your husband's death." I told her what I suspected, and I explained that it wasn't enough yet to take to the police.

When I was finished with my summary, I asked: "What would you like me to do?"

"Get the bastards," she replied. "I'll pay whatever it takes."

***

I spent the early part of the afternoon requesting all the public records I could think of that might be useful to the case.

Public records requests are central to the work of journalists and investigators. In New Hampshire, they're governed by a state law known as RSA 91-A, the Right to Know Law.

Requests have to be submitted in writing to the agency that oversees the information. One good thing about New Hampshire's law is that it requires agencies to supply the requested information within five business days, unless there are extenuating circumstances that prevent this rapid turnaround. I've heard of journalists and citizen's advocacy groups waiting several months for their requests to be fulfilled in other states.

I emailed the state Department of Administrative Services and requested copies of all invoices submitted by Tree Kings for its work on behalf of the state, going back for the last six years. I also asked for any other records related to the fulfillment of Tree Kings' state contract, including emails, state filings or reports, and any other relevant documentation. Finally, I requested all documents and correspondence pertaining to Donovan Forestry Services' challenge of Tree Kings' contract and the subsequent investigation, including emails and memos.

I specified that the records could be delivered electronically or in print, whichever was easiest.

At quarter past two, I left my apartment for my three p.m. meeting with Tree Kings.

* * *

The forest management company's headquarters were located on Route 132 in the northeast quadrant of Concord. The property was surrounded by a high chain link fence topped with barbed wire. I felt like I was approaching the Kennedy compound as I drove through the front gate.

In the center of the lot stood a large, two-story building. The building's main entrance was located on the left, and to the right of this entrance were several garage bay doors. A fleet of forestry equipment and heavy machinery for cutting and removing trees was distributed on either side of the building.

I parked in front of the main entrance and headed inside.

I don't know what I was expecting to see when I entered the lobby—wood paneling? A metal reception desk that resembled an oil tanker?—but the image I was greeted with was very different from what I imagined.

There was a reception desk, all right, but it was made of a premium, high-quality wood, perhaps ash or maple. The design of the reception area was very modern and elegant, with light gray carpeting and glass doors leading from the lobby to an interior hallway. The place seemed more like a psychiatrist's office than a forestry company.

Hammond was nothing if not image-conscious, I noted.

While the décor didn't match my expectations, the receptionist did. She was a hardened woman who looked to be about sixty but was probably at least ten years younger than that, with nicotine-stained fingers and long, lacquered nails. The nails were painted the same shade of electric blue as her mascara.

"I'm Parker Hanson. I have a three o'clock appointment to see Mr. Hammond?"

"Have a seat." She pointed toward a row of stylish chairs along the wall.

I sat down and picked up a magazine from the small wooden table beside my chair. I was amused to find Hammond's smiling face gracing the cover.

I had been waiting for less than a minute when a short, well-dressed young woman in a cream-colored suit and high heels appeared. "Mr. Hanson? I'm Monica Wyman," she said, offering me her hand. "Mr. Hammond is just wrapping up another meeting, but I can show you around our facility in the meantime."

She handed me her business card as she led me through the glass doors and into the hallway. Printed in gold lettering were the words, "Monica Wyman, Vice President of Marketing and Communications." In spite of her lofty position with the company, she looked like she was about to graduate from college that weekend.

Ms. Wyman gave me a tour of the building, about half of which consisted of office space for sales and administration. The other half comprised a massive garage used for maintenance and repairs of the company's forestry equipment, with a small team of full-time mechanics. I made a show of taking pictures with my cell phone for the "story" I was working on.

During the course of the tour, I learned that Tree Kings provided forest management services to private landowners as well. But its contract with the state accounted for some two-thirds of its revenue.

I also learned enough about the field of forest management to write a whole series of articles, if I were still a journalist.

"More than eight out of every ten acres in New Hampshire is covered by trees," Ms. Wyman said. "In fact, we're the second-leading state in the country in terms of the percentage of forested land. This landscape has a huge effect on the environment, as well as our state's economy. According to a recent study, forest-based recreational activities like hiking, mountain biking, hunting, and ATV use contribute more than three billion dollars each year to our state economy—while industries like logging and biofuel generate another billion and a half in income."

"Wow, I had no idea."

"Yeah, most people don't realize how essential our forests are to preserving our way of life. They're also crucial for mitigating the effects of climate change, such as the higher frequency of extreme weather events we now experience. Trees help remove carbon from our atmosphere through a process known as sequestration. While older forests generally store more carbon per acre than younger ones do, younger trees typically sequester carbon at a faster rate. That's one reason why it's important to have a healthy, diverse forest ecosystem, with a mix of younger and older tree stands. Yet, New Hampshire has seen a net loss of more than one hundred twenty-six thousand acres of forest land overall from 1983 to 2017. That's nearly a three-percent reduction during that time."

"So what do you do to ensure the health of the state's forests? How do you accomplish that goal?"

"Well, there are many aspects involved. The first step is

to collect information about the various forest populations. We use GIS data, but most of our activity involves field work. For instance, we do what we call 'timber cruises,' where we measure the average tree size, volume, age, and condition of a stand using representative trees. We're assessing not just the health but also the diversity of the trees. And we're looking for signs of disease or invasive species."

She continued: "We use a practice called silviculture to maintain the health of the forests. It's basically a fancy term for controlling the growth, composition, and structure of a forest stand. There are two main approaches you can take: even-aged management, in which you're trying to create a uniform age to the forest, or uneven-aged management, where you want trees at different stages of life. The approach you might take depends on factors like the composition of a forest and how much light its trees require. An even-aged forest will have a single canopy, while in an uneven-aged forest, the younger trees will grow in the shade of the older ones. To create an even-aged forest, you might clear-cut entire sections of forest to allow for uniform new growth. For an uneven-aged forest, you might remove individual trees to allow for new growth amid the existing trees.

"As our foresters are assessing a timber stand, they're marking trees to be removed, either because the trees are diseased or to make room for new growth. Our loggers then cut down the marked trees and sell the timber for use as lumber or biofuel. We pass on this revenue to the state to offset some of the cost of managing the forest, and we keep a small percentage for ourselves.

"We also look to control and remove invasive plants and insects that can harm the forests. Insects like the emerald ash borer can devastate trees by tunneling under the bark. This tunneling reduces the tree's ability to move water and nutrients, ultimately weakening it. Invasive plants like glossy buckthorn outcompete the surrounding vegetation for light and other resources, which also weakens the trees. We remove invasive plants and spray herbicide and insecticide to control the spread of these threats to the forest ecosystem."

"How many employees do you have overall?" I asked her.

"We have six certified foresters who collect data, prescribe plans of action, and mark trees for removal. They work all around the state, including for our private clients. We also employ three four-member logging crews who fell, stack, and remove trees. We have a handful of people spraying trees and removing invasive underbrush, depending on the season; right now is the busiest time for spraying, actually. We have two full-time mechanics on staff to service all our equipment, as we have well over a million dollars invested in heavy machinery. And we have about a dozen office employees who handle sales, marketing, and administration. Altogether, I'd say we employ close to forty people."

Ms. Wyman led me through the garage and around the grounds, where she pointed out the various equipment and its uses.

The machines included a "feller buncher," which was a motorized vehicle that looked like an excavator, except instead of a bucket for scooping earth, the arm contained an attachment for grabbing and cutting trees at their base. There were also a few harvesters, which could pick up fallen trees, strip them of their limbs, and cut them into neat, uniform-sized logs in seconds; log loaders for picking up processed logs and stacking them on trucks for removal; mulchers with high-speed rotating blades that could shred small trees and underbrush like tissue paper; a stump grinder; and a few wood chippers.

"The disc blades on our mulchers rotate at speeds between one and two thousand times a second," she boasted.

I also noticed the box truck I'd seen before, parked behind the company's main facility, next to two huge trailers for hauling the heavy machinery.

We finished the tour outside Hammond's office on the second floor of the building. Ms. Wyman knocked on the brass-plated door, and Hammond let us in.

Hammond was a tall man, at least six foot two, who looked to be in his mid-fifties but was still very fit. His short, blond hair was in the process of turning silver. He had a naturally tanned face, as if he spent a lot of time outdoors. He was wearing a cobalt-colored blazer, a cornflower blue button-down shirt, and pleated khaki pants.

The windows in Hammond's corner office afforded a view of the Merrimack River and, beyond it, downtown Concord on one side and nothing but woods on the other. The office was furnished with a cherry wood desk, leather chairs, and a large leather sofa. Numerous hunting trophies adorned the walls, including the heads of deer, a bobcat, and even a grizzly bear.

Ms. Wyman led the introductions, then excused herself and left, closing the door behind her.

"Sit down and make yourself comfortable," Hammond said, gesturing toward the sofa. "Would you like a drink?"

"No, thank you."

Taking an old fashioned glass from a mini bar in the corner of the office, he dropped in two sugar cubes, an orange slice, and a maraschino cherry. He added a few drops of bitters to the sugar cubes and the fruit, then mashed the mixture with a pestle. After filling the glass with ice and Wild Turkey rye whiskey, he sat down in one of the chairs opposite the sofa.

"So," Hammond said, leaning back in his chair as he swirled his drink, "I trust Monica was helpful in providing what you needed?"

"Yes, she was."

"What else would you like to know?"

"Before we begin, do you mind if I take some photos of you in your office for my story?"

"Let's save the photos for the end."

"Sure, of course. It's quite an operation you've built," I said, gesturing around me. "But I'm curious: Why get into forest management? It seems like a strange choice for an Ivy League business graduate."

He smiled. "I was always fascinated by big, loud machinery as a child. I guess this was a way for me to satisfy that interest as an adult. Plus, we're helping to take care of our natural resources. As you can see from my many trophies on the wall, I'm an avid outdoorsman myself. I've always enjoyed spending time in nature, which is what got me hooked on hunting as a teenager. I love the thrill of the chase, but just as importantly, I love being outside in the woods. And hey, business is business. It beats being bored to tears working on Wall Street."

"Yeah, but you must have a lot of expenses to worry about: heavy equipment, supplies, and labor costs, not to mention gasoline, parts, and insurance. Seems like there would be easier ways to make money."

"Well, money isn't my sole objective. We provide a valuable service for the state. We're supporting the economies of our local communities, and we're helping to be responsible stewards of the environment. As I'm sure you're aware, I also own a few other businesses. But this is what you might call my 'passion project'—and I would say we're doing quite well."

"I'm sure you are. On second thought, I think I will have a drink after all. Do you mind if I help myself?"

"No, go ahead."

I got up and walked over to the bar, taking the opportunity to glance around the office as I did so.

"Aside from your contract with the state, Ms. Wyman said that about a third of your business comes from private landowners. What would a typical client look like?"

"Some are conservation trusts or other organizations looking to manage their land responsibly. Others are families who own large tracts of forest land and want to earn money from their investment by harvesting some of the timber sustainably."

While he was talking, I poured myself a club soda and added a lemon wedge. As I looked around the office, I noticed on Hammond's desk there was a red baseball cap with the letters "AXA" written across the front in black.

Alpha Chi Alpha. Presumably a memento from Hammond's fraternity experience at Dartmouth.

"You got your undergraduate degree in economics from Dartmouth, right? What year did you graduate again?

"Class of ninety-three."

In my capacity as a reporter for the *Herald*, I had learned many things. One of those things was that New Hampshire Governor Jack Gordon had graduated from Dartmouth College in 1991, just two years before Hammond.

Another was that Gordon had also been a member of Alpha Chi Alpha.

Gordon and Hammond were in the same fraternity together.

At the same time.

When I shared this realization with Hammond, his reaction wasn't at all what I expected.

"Now it's time for me to ask *you* a question, Mr. Hanson," he said, his tone changing dramatically. "Why did you lie to me about being a reporter—and what is it you're *really* after?"

* * *

Hammond's response surprised me. It also suggested he knew the real purpose for my visit.

"What do you mean?"

"I know you're not on assignment for *New Hampshire Magazine*. I called the editorial department there, and they said they'd never heard of you. I also know you happen to be a private investigator. I Googled you before this meeting and found your third-rate website buried on the ninth page of the search results. What I don't know is, why did you go through this whole charade to talk with me? What are you investigating?"

I thought about what had happened to Mark and Maggie. "That's between my client and me."

When I had called Monica Wyman to set up the interview with Hammond, I debated whether to give my real name or a pseudonym. I decided to use my real name, because if Hammond or anyone else on his staff Googled me, they would see a long list of *Herald* stories with my byline. I figured that would reassure them I was a legitimate journalist.

But I wasn't counting on Hammond calling the publication I'd used for my cover, or clicking through so many search results that he'd found the poorly advertised website for my private investigator business, which admittedly didn't rank highly in Google's search algorithm. Usually, web searchers gave up after looking through only the first two or three pages of search results.

Hammond was a shrewd adversary, I realized—and I wouldn't underestimate him again.

Unfortunately, this realization came too late. Hammond already knew who I was.

Just as importantly, he knew that I understood there was a clear connection between him and Gordon.

"It's time for you to leave, Mr. Hanson, before I call security."

That was my cue. He didn't have to ask me twice.

* * *

My encounter with Hammond had taken place on Friday afternoon. Barely twelve hours later, those two goons had broken into my apartment and tried to kill me.

Now, as I sat alone in the all-night diner near the Manchester Airport at five o'clock on Saturday morning, waiting for my early breakfast order to arrive, I considered everything I knew so far.

The owner of Tree Kings and the governor of New Hampshire not only went to college together; they were fraternity brothers during their time at Dartmouth. That's a bond that lasts for life.

Several years later, Hammond's company repeatedly wins a state contract in questionable fashion over a key business rival. There's evidence to suggest the bidding might have been rigged, but it's conveniently explained away—and the matter is quickly dismissed.

A member of the governor's staff asks the press to investigate. Soon thereafter, both the reporter and the staff member perish under highly suspicious circumstances.

The critical question was, did Governor Jack Gordon play a direct role in these events? Did he have any knowledge of the alleged fraud in the state procurement office, or the murders that I strongly suspected Hammond had ordered to cover up this crime?

The waitress on the overnight shift set a plate of steaming food down in front of me. She looked as tired as I must have looked at that point, though maybe not as shell-shocked.

Narrowly avoiding one's death can do that to a person.

"Need anything else, hon?" she asked.

"No, I'm good. Thanks."

In addition to my omelet, the plate contained sourdough toast with strawberry jam. I took a bite of toast and chewed slowly and deliberately, trying to calm my still-jangling nerves.

The jam was surprisingly good, especially for all-night diner fare.

Regarding my investigation into Mark's and Maggie's deaths, I was in a pretty big jam of my own. And I wasn't really sure what to do.

Walking away from the case wasn't an option. Brooke needed my help, and I wasn't about to abandon her just because the seas had gotten choppier.

But I'd never been in a situation like this before. This case was much bigger and more dangerous than anything I'd taken on previously.

I was facing a powerful band of enemies with the weight of an entire state government behind them, and I was worried I'd leaped headlong into the waves without knowing how to swim.

There was only one thing to do, I realized as I dug into my omelet.

Start paddling.

Chapter 6

After finishing my breakfast, I returned to my hotel room and slept until noon. When I woke up, I took a quick shower and got ready for Mark's funeral.

Remembering that I had two memorial services to attend that weekend, I'd had the foresight to pack a dark blue suit before leaving my apartment.

I got dressed in a plain white button-down shirt and my suit, put on a navy-blue-and-gold striped tie, and drove to the Immaculate Conception Parish Church in north Concord. There were so many cars already jammed into the Catholic church's parking lot that I had to park on the street.

The inside of the church was packed as well, but I was able to slip into a pew near the back. I spotted Brooke in the front pew with her two young children: Dominic, age eight, and Daisy, age five.

Brooke had told me about her children during the initial meeting we had to discuss her case. Although I guess I'd understood on some abstract level how devastating their father's death must have been for them, seeing the pained and somewhat distant looks on their faces really drove home the enormity of the entire family's loss.

The service itself was quite moving. I didn't know Mark at

all and had never actually met him. But from the kind words and remembrances of those who spoke, it was evident that he'd touched many people's lives.

Brooke told a story about the family's annual vacations on Newfound Lake and how Mark would entertain them around the campfire with slapstick comedy routines. In one recurring bit, which he called "The Beetles," he would sing a Beatles song as if he were Lennon or McCartney and then fall on his back halfway through the song and flail his arms and legs helplessly, like he couldn't right himself.

"Dominic and Daisy were too young to understand Mark's bizarre sense of humor. They had no idea what he was doing or why, but they found his physical comedy hilarious," Brooke said. "Afterwards, we'd sit around the fire and eat s'mores while we listened to the sound of the loons calling from across the lake. But I always felt like we had our own loon sitting right there with us."

Brooke's story made me realize what a huge hole Mark's death had left in the family's lives. As I listened to her speak, I resolved in my mind to bring Mark's killer to justice—no matter the cost.

But I felt like I needed to do something more for her children as well.

Although the church didn't pass around a collection plate during the service, there was a box set up for donations, and I saw many people put in bills and coins as they passed by. Looking at the donation box, I thought of a small gesture I could make for Dominic and Daisy.

Maybe it was a little hokey, but at least it was something.

When the service was over, I approached Brooke and offered my condolences again. "How much do your children know about what happened to their dad?" I asked.

"They know Mark was killed in a car accident. That's all."

I told her what I was thinking and asked if she thought it would be okay. She said yes and told me when the children had been born.

I also shared my idea with the priest and told him I would make a generous donation if I had his blessing. He gave me the go-ahead and opened the donation box for me. I looked through the coins, and by chance I found two that were minted in the same years that Dominic and Daisy were born.

I took the two coins and replaced them with a twenty-dollar bill. Then I went up to the children and introduced myself.

"You don't know me," I said, "but I was a friend of your dad. I was also with him when he died, and he wanted you to have these coins. They have the years you were born stamped on them, and he kept them in his pocket wherever he went to remind him of you both. He asked me to give them to you. Now, you can hold onto these coins as a way to remember *him*. He loved you both very much."

The children took the coins as if they were magical talismans. I saw Brooke smile and nod her appreciation, and I nodded back.

* * *

Before I left the church, there was something else I wanted to do. I was hoping Mark's boss, Chief of Staff Bryce Kilcullen, would be at the service as well—and I wasn't disappointed. I'd done some Internet research on him, and he was easy enough to spot among the crowd.

Kilcullen was in his early forties, with fair hair parted on the side and wire-rimmed glasses. Unlike Gordon and Hammond, he had attended Yale, where he'd graduated with a degree in political science. At Mark's funeral, he was wearing a black silk suit that probably cost more than my entire wardrobe and a scarlet-and-black striped tie.

I approached Kilcullen and introduced myself. "Mark worked for you, didn't he?"

"Yes, that's right. He was a very valued employee, and I was devastated to learn of his loss."

There was nothing in Kilcullen's manner to suggest he was lying. But I wanted to know more, so I continued with my questions.

"Mark told me he'd raised concerns about possible fraud in the state's procurement process, but you dismissed what he had to say. Why was that?"

Again, there was no perceptible reaction to what I said. Either Kilcullen really did have no knowledge of any fraud, or he was one cool customer.

"I didn't dismiss his concerns. In fact, I took them quite seriously. I looked into them, and they proved to be nothing in the end."

"Mark didn't believe that. Did you know he was working with a reporter from the *Herald* when the two of them were killed?"

"No, I wasn't aware of that. Who did you say you were?"

"I'm a friend of the family."

"Look, I don't like to speak ill of the dead, but the truth was, Mark could be a little bit of a conspiracy theorist. I personally handled the investigation into Mark's concerns. I even gave the state procurement director a lie detector test—which he passed, by the way—and I can verify that there was nothing more to the complaint than the rumblings of a disgruntled loser."

"Do you happen to have the results of that polygraph test?"

"No. I considered the matter closed, so I threw them away. Listen, I don't mean to be rude, but I need to pay my respects to Ms. Bowman and then head out. Being chief of staff to the governor means there are no days off. I'm sure you can understand."

"Of course. Thanks for your time."

As I watched him make his way through the crowd toward Brooke, I wondered if the nugget about the polygraph test was true. I also wondered how I might chat with the head of procurement for the state of New Hampshire myself.

* * *

I left the church and drove straight to Scott's Shots in Hooksett to meet with Travis Tanner. It was just after four o'clock as I was parking. I grabbed the summons from the glove compartment of my rental car and headed into the bar.

I had left my coat and tie in the car, but I was still the best-dressed person in the place by a wide margin. I could feel peoples' eyes following me, making it clear that I stood out as a foreigner in this environment.

I sat at the bar and ordered a Cape Codder. "But hold the vodka," I told the bartender.

"Coulda just ordered a cranberry juice," she said with a smirk.

"Where's the fun in that?"

I scanned the bar and saw Tanner talking with some friends in one corner. He saw me as well and came over to me with a mug of cheap draft beer in his hand. "You that detective guy?"

"I am. Thanks for coming."

I handed him the summons and told him he'd been served.

"What's this?"

"It's a notice to appear in court. Your ex-girlfriend is suing you for lack of child support. Listen," I added, placing a hand on his shoulder, "I know you don't know me at all, but if I could give you some advice: Be there for your kid. Make your required payments, yes, but get involved in your child's life as well. I don't think you know how important that is or how much it will mean to your child in the end."

I had no idea if my words would have any effect. And I didn't harbor any illusions that they would. But I felt like I had to try.

I downed my cranberry juice, dropped a five-dollar bill on the bar, and got up to leave.

"So what about Kim?" Tanner said. "She's not here, then? When do I get to see her?"

He still hasn't caught on, I realized.

If Tanner hadn't blown off his responsibility as a parent—and if I hadn't just come from a funeral where I was reminded that two other young children had recently lost their own father forever—I might have felt sorry for him.

* * *

I left Scott's Shots and drove to another bar, the Tipsy Moose in Manchester, where I was hoping to see my downstairs neighbor, Amalia.

The Tipsy Moose had a very different vibe than Scott's. It was much more upscale, with laminate wood floors, fashionable wooden stools with metal legs, a faux brick backdrop to the bar, and clothing and other merchandise for sale. The wait staff were all fully clothed as well, unlike at Scott's—and there were a few dozen craft beers from local microbreweries available on tap or in cans. I didn't feel out of place wearing a suit.

It was just before five o'clock, and the Saturday evening crowd hadn't yet arrived. I found a seat at the bar, and Amalia greeted me with a fist bump.

"*Hola*, neighbor."

I ordered a seltzer water with a lime and, because I hadn't eaten anything since my early morning breakfast at the diner some twelve hours earlier, a chopped salad with no bacon.

I also told Amalia about those two thugs who'd tried to eighty-six me in my sleep the night before.

"If you see a couple of strange guys hanging around the apartment building, you might want to let the police know," I said. "In the meantime, I'm staying at a hotel here in Manchester until this whole thing blows over."

"Look at you, hitting the big time!" she joked. "If you need any backup, let me know."

"Thanks. I appreciate that. For now, if you could just collect my mail, I'd be forever grateful."

"Sure, no problem. Can I ask why you have a contract out on your head?"

"I'm still trying to figure that out for myself. But I think it might have something to do with possible fraud in our state government."

The guy sitting next to me at the bar, a wispy young man wearing an "Amyl and the Sniffers" tee shirt and drinking a wild berry hard seltzer, must have been listening to our conversation, because he said: "Oh, they're all corrupt!"

"Who's all corrupt?"

"Politicians. All of 'em."

I'm sure it was intended to be a harmless throwaway line in a bar. But his outburst touched a sensitive nerve for me as a former investigative reporter.

"Yeah, I totally get why you feel that way," I said, turning toward him. "All too often, it seems like our elected officials are looking out for their own best interests and not ours. But not all government employees are corrupt, and that kind of cynicism actually hurts our democratic process. It provides cover for the truly corrupt ones to keep gaming the system. If we think all politicians are crooks, that gives us an excuse to just ignore the corruption—or worse, to not vote at all. If we want a democracy that actually works for everyone and not just the rich and the powerful, then we need to pay attention to the news, engage in the democratic process, and hold government officials accountable when they break the law."

"Hmmph." The guy rolled his eyes at me, took his can of hard seltzer, and moved to a table by the wall.

"Nice work, Bernie," Amalia said. "I can see why someone wanted you dead. If you chase off any more of my customers by talking about politics, *I'm* going to shoot you myself."

"Sorry. I'll try to stick to sports from now on."

A waitress brought my chopped salad out from the kitchen, and I began eating while Mal tended to her other customers.

The Red Sox were playing the Dodgers again in a game that had started at four o'clock, Eastern time. I watched as Shohei Ohtani singlehandedly dismantled the Sox by pitching seven shutout innings and hitting two home runs. Not since the legendary Babe Ruth had a player been so dominant as both a pitcher *and* a hitter.

The Dodgers won, 4-1.

I finished my nonalcoholic seltzer water, said goodbye to Mal, and left the bar.

* * *

Before returning to my hotel room for the evening, I drove by my apartment building to see if I could spot my attackers from the night before.

I was assuming they weren't finished with me yet and would be watching the building to make another attempt on my life. I was also guessing that McDougal and his partner, the two Manchester detectives who'd responded to my call, had better things to do than to set up camp in my neighborhood and watch for my assailants.

If I wanted them off my back, I figured I was going to have to do the job myself.

I circled the block slowly three times, but I didn't see anything suspicious. None of the cars on the street were occupied, and nobody was hanging around on the sidewalks.

Swing and a miss.

Chapter 7

I woke up around seven o'clock the next morning. I got dressed, grabbed a Sunday paper from the hotel lobby, and walked over to the diner again for breakfast, where I ordered another egg white omelet and black decaf coffee.

Although I routinely read most of my news online—I had subscriptions to the digital editions of the *Washington Post* for national and international news, as well as the *Herald* for state political news and the *New Hampshire Union Leader* out of Manchester for local information—I still liked to read the Sunday print editions whenever I could.

There was something warmly nostalgic about flipping through the various sections over breakfast and getting ink stains all over your fingers. I liked reading the Sunday comics as well. In a fast-paced world with so many changes, it was oddly comforting to see that Blondie was still mad at Dagwood for not helping with the chores, Garfield still hated Mondays, and Snoopy was still flying missions behind enemy lines in his Sopwith Camel.

The Sundays that began without a print newspaper in my hands weren't nearly as enjoyable.

After a leisurely breakfast with the newspaper, I returned to my hotel room. I opened my laptop and sought to learn more about David Lemay, the director of procurement for the state of New Hampshire government.

For most people, social media is a way to connect with others and keep them informed. For investigators, it's like exploring the attractions at Disneyland.

Within five minutes, I had found Lemay's Facebook page and learned that he was a classic car enthusiast who owned a cherry red 1967 Mustang convertible. He took the vehicle to car shows throughout New England, where he displayed it proudly. He'd even won a few trophies, which he also showcased in his social media feeds.

Lemay was in the process of building a second classic car, a 1970 Plymouth Superbird. In his most recent Facebook post, he noted that he was looking for original popup headlight assemblies for the car. "When I started building this car, I didn't realize how hard it would be to find parts!" he wrote in his post.

I didn't know much about classic cars. But I knew someone who did. Burt, the retired chiropractor who was in my cardiac rehab group, was also a gearhead.

I had an idea for how I could talk with Lemay without inviting suspicion about my motives, and maybe even steal a glimpse into his finances. But I would need Burt's help to pull it off.

Normally, I would have just waited until I saw Burt at cardiac rehab the next day. But the plan I had in mind required immediate action. I found Burt's phone number in an online directory and gave him a call.

"There's someone I need to talk to for an investigation, but I'm worried that a direct approach will just scare him off," I explained. "The guy's interested in classic cars, and I thought that might be a way for me to get access to him. But hot rods aren't my area of expertise."

"You want my help in working undercover?" Burt said. "Count me in!"

I told Burt what Lemay was looking for and said that if I could track down those headlight assemblies first, I could offer Lemay the parts myself. "How do I do that?" I asked.

Burt said he usually looks on eBay first when he's in the market for classic car parts. With Burt's guidance, I searched on eBay but was unable to find what I was looking for.

Burt then told me about some other websites run by classic car aficionados that he turns to when he isn't successful on eBay. On the "Parts for Sale" section of a website called PACRAT, which stood for "Parts and Cars for Regular Auto Tuners" (and whose motto was: "Show us your junk!"), we saw that someone calling himself "HotRodStewart" had the parts Lemay needed.

I sent a private direct message to HotRodStewart, who lived in North Carolina. A few minutes later, I got a response saying he could ship the parts to me for arrival on Tuesday. I used Venmo to pay him.

When the transaction was completed, I contacted Lemay online. I told him I had the headlight assemblies he wanted. I mentioned that I was local and could deliver the parts to him in person Tuesday evening if he wanted to write me a check. Burt agreed to go with me and help maintain my cover as a fellow car enthusiast.

By now, it was almost noon. The wheels of my plan set in motion, I showered, put on my dark blue suit again, and left for Maggie's service.

* * *

Maggie's memorial service was very different from Mark's. It was a nontraditional service held on the beach in the small coastal town of Rye, a place that held a special meaning for Maggie. She loved to surf on her days off from the newspaper, and she would engage in this activity year-round—even braving the frigid waters during the depths of the New England winters.

At Rye Beach, Maggie had discovered an entire community of surfers who shared her passion. New Hampshire might not seem like a big surfing destination, but Rye Beach has an exposed reef break that results in pretty consistent waves, making it a popular location for surfers across the Northeast.

From Manchester, I drove east on Route 101 and turned onto Route 111, taking that road almost all the way out to the coast. Shortly before Route 111 intersected in a "T" with Route 1A along the coastline, I turned right onto Sea Road so that I would have a slightly longer drive along the shore.

From Sea Road, I turned north onto Route 1A and took in the stunning views on the final leg up to Rye Beach: multimillion-dollar mansions on the left-hand side of the road and ocean expanse on the right.

When I arrived at Rye Beach, I felt overdressed for the occasion—even though I hadn't bothered to wear a tie. Most of the attendees were dressed in shorts and sandals, and there were about a dozen surfers clad in thick neoprene body suits and carrying surfboards.

Conrad Bellows was the only other person I saw wearing a suit on the beach. I said hello to him and to a few other former colleagues from the *Herald*.

I also spotted Callie among the crowd. She was wearing an attractive blue-and-white sun dress that showed off her tanned figure. She smiled and waved when she saw me, and I joined her and said hello.

Callie introduced me to Maggie's parents, Brendan and Faye.

"I'm so sorry for your loss," I told them. "Your daughter was the bravest and best reporter the newspaper had."

"You worked with her, then?" Brendan asked.

"Yes, until a few years ago."

The nondenominational service was led by a Unitarian Universalist minister, who fittingly read Shakespeare's sonnet about death that begins:

> *Like as the waves make towards the pebbled shore,*
> *So do our minutes hasten to their end;*
> *Each changing place with that which goes before,*
> *In sequent toil all forwards do contend.*

Family and friends also shared their fondest memories of Maggie. I was already familiar with some of the stories, but many of them I'd never heard before.

Although the sun was shining, there was a strong coastal breeze, and I noticed that Callie shivered at one point during the service. I took off my suit jacket and offered it to her.

"Thank you," she said, and she put on the jacket. "I know this is very last minute, but Maggie and I had tickets to see a dance performance at the Capitol Center this evening, and I don't want to go by myself. Would you like to join me?"

"Sure," I said. "Sounds like fun."

At the end of the memorial service, Maggie's surfer friends got on their boards and paddled out to sea. Each of them carried a small container holding some of Maggie's ashes.

When they were about a hundred yards from the shore, they stopped and spread her ashes among the waves. The crying of the seagulls and the low moaning of the surf lapping against the sand set an appropriate tone for saying goodbye.

* * *

The performance I'd agreed to attend with Callie began at five o'clock, which gave us both enough time to return home and rinse off the salt coating our skin from the sea coast air before the show. Because we would be approaching the Capitol Center for the Arts in Concord from opposite directions, we decided to meet in front of the theater at a quarter to five.

The show featured a professional dance troupe out of Portsmouth called Social Movement. According to the program, they were an eight-member contemporary dance company whose performances explored societal issues and injustices through movement and physicality.

"Contemporary dance blends elements of different styles, like ballet, jazz, and lyrical," Callie explained as we took our seats and awaited the performance. "It isn't restricted by the rules governing traditional dance forms. Instead, there's fluidity and freedom of movement, which lets the dancers communicate abstract ideas and evoke certain emotions."

The show consisted of a string of vignettes, each one conveying a theme such as poverty, hunger, racism, and xenophobia. Each vignette spotlighted a different dancer who began with a solo and then was joined by the rest of the group.

The dancers' movements were beautiful, graceful, powerful, and evocative. I can't say I understood what they were trying to express the whole time, but I got the gist of most of the performance.

"Did you notice the interplay between the dancers?" Callie said excitedly when the show was over. "Depending on their movements, the supporting dancers were either allies or obstacles to the main character in each story. And this dynamic sometimes shifted in mid-dance. Like, the idea seemed to be that we all have the capacity to either help or hinder each other."

"You have such a passion for dance. It's great to see," I said. "I would think after dancing all week you'd want nothing to do with dance in your spare time. Like how carpenters are supposedly terrible at doing projects around the house, because the last thing they want to do on their day off is swing a hammer."

"Oh, no. For me, it's a chance to see other ideas and forms of expression. I can take those ideas and apply them within my own choreography. I learn something new every time I watch a performance."

Because we were hungry, we walked to a Thai food restaurant a few blocks north of the theater. We sat at a table outside, and Callie asked our waiter for a glass of Riesling. I ordered the chicken with green curry sauce, and she had the pad Thai.

"So, is Callie short for anything?" I asked her.

"Yes, actually—Calliope."

"The Greek muse of singing and epic poetry."

She looked surprised. "How do you know that?"

"The benefits of a classical education," I said, quoting Hans Gruber from *Die Hard*.

"My mother is a classics professor at UNH," she said, almost apologetically.

"A-ha! That explains it. And your father?"

"He's a lawyer. They're divorced."

"How did you become interested in dancing?"

"It's probably a common story, but I was inspired by seeing *The Nutcracker* as a young girl. Our family would go every year during Thanksgiving weekend. It's one of the few happy memories I have of us all together. My older brother died when I was eight, and my parents got divorced soon after."

"I'm so sorry to hear that. That must have been tough."

"What about you? How did you become a journalist?"

"When I first got to college, I thought I wanted to be a doctor. It wasn't until later that I had any idea about journalism. I needed a course to fulfill a writing requirement in the second semester of my freshman year, and I took a class with this professor, Harlan Rhodes. He had this way of bringing the subject to life and making it seem so … I don't know—*exciting*, I guess, and also noble at the same time. I used to think of journalism as kind of dull, but he totally transformed my way of looking at the world. He would talk about how Edward R. Murrow used to fly on Allied bombing raids in Europe during World War II, and how his first-person accounts—delivered at great personal risk—kept Americans informed of what was happening during the war. He would tell these stories, and I was totally mesmerized. Right there, I decided to switch my major from biology to communications."

"And now you're a private detective."

"Yeah. Now I mostly expose cheating spouses and serve people court summonses."

"The case you're working on now is important, though."

"Yes. This case is definitely important."

"That was a nice memorial service for Maggie today. Do you

think you'll catch the people who killed her?"

Her lips quivered as she said the words. I took her hands in mine and said, "I promise."

* * *

After we'd finished dinner, I walked Callie to her car.

"Thank you for coming to the performance with me," she said. "If you hadn't, I think I would have just stayed home."

"Your sister wasn't available?"

"She and her husband had other plans."

"Well, I'm glad I came. I had a really nice time."

"Me, too."

It was after nine o'clock in the evening, and the orange glow from the street lights seemed to cast a halo around Callie's long, brown hair.

I wondered what it would be like to kiss her. But I didn't think it would be appropriate so soon after her roommate's death. Although there were definitely sparks between us, I didn't want to take advantage of her emotional vulnerability at the moment.

Callie got into her car, put on her seat belt, and drove away with a smile and a wave. I watched her car's tail lights grow smaller as they receded into the night. Then I walked back to my own car, still smiling from my memory of the evening.

Like I'd done the night before, I drove past my apartment building on the way back to my hotel to see if I could catch a glimpse of those two goons who'd tried to kill me.

The neighborhood was dead quiet. But there was no sign of my attackers, either.

Strike two.

Maybe Hammond was a thoughtful employer who gave his assassins their weekends off? I wondered if they got dental coverage and a matching 401(k) as well.

If so, that would give the phrase "the woke mob" a whole new meaning.

Chapter 8

Monday morning's cardiac rehab session was marked by a discussion of how incredibly talented—and unique—Shohei Ohtani was as a baseball player and how there were no other comparable stars among his generation. He'd hit another home run in Sunday's game, and it proved to be the difference in the score as the Dodgers had won, 4-3.

"Ohtani destroyed us," Joe said. "The guy's not even human."

"League MVP for sure," Mickey added.

When the rehab session was over, I drove from the hospital up to the Concord Police Department to see Detective Connor.

After those two hitmen had tried to kill me, I figured it was time to bring the police up to speed on everything that had happened, even though I still didn't have any hard evidence to back up my suspicions.

The murders of Maggie and Mark had taken place in Concord. I had a prior relationship with Connor as well, so he seemed like the logical choice to confide in.

"Hanson, to what do I owe the pleasure?" he said sarcastically when he saw me, popping a couple of Smarties into his mouth. "Is this about that woman whose apartment was ransacked?"

"In a way. Got a minute?"

We retreated to a small conference room, where I walked him through the events of the previous week, starting with my initial meeting with Brooke and ending with my escapade early Saturday morning.

"And you didn't think to mention any of this to me when I responded to the break-in at your friend's apartment?"

"I'm mentioning it to you now. Besides, I didn't know yet about Maggie's investigation when the break-in occurred."

"So, how do you think this all ties together?"

"I'm not sure, but I strongly suspect that someone—or possibly multiple people—within Governor Gordon's administration rigged the bidding process so that Hammond's forestry company would continue to win the contract to manage the state's forest lands. Either these people, or Hammond, or most likely both parties also had Mark and Maggie killed to keep this alleged fraud under wraps. They also tossed Maggie's apartment to remove whatever evidence she might have collected for her story, and they tried to kill me when they found out I was looking into the contract as well."

"Why do you assume the attack on you is related to what the *Herald* reporter was working on? You do seem to piss a lot of people off."

"Present company included?"

"No comment."

"It's too much of a coincidence not to be related. And I'll tell you one other thing as well. During my meeting with Hammond, as soon as I brought up the fact that I knew he and the governor had been fraternity brothers at Dartmouth together, that's when his attitude *really* changed. Like he wasn't happy I knew about that connection."

"So what are you saying? You think the governor of our state is personally involved in the crimes you were just describing? That's nuts."

"Think about it—"

"I don't *have* to think about it, Hanson. There are a million reasons Hammond could have been upset that don't implicate the governor in a crime. Maybe he didn't want people unfairly thinking his company was getting preferential treatment from the state because he and the governor were buddies once in college, for chrissakes."

I didn't have a response, so I stayed quiet.

* * *

Connor said he'd push to consider the accident that killed Mark and Maggie as a homicide. He also promised to link that investigation with the break-in at Maggie's and Callie's apartment, focusing on possible connections to Tree Kings and Hammond.

I was glad Connor was taking those steps. But it was clear I was going to have to produce some solid evidence myself if I wanted him to take my suspicions about the governor seriously.

When I got back to my hotel room, I submitted another Right to Know request for public records, this time asking for information about all visitors to Governor Gordon's office during the last three years. I thought maybe I could establish a more recent connection between Gordon and Hammond if I could prove that Hammond had been to the governor's office during that period.

I also looked online to see if I could find any further links between the two men. I did a regular Google search for the names "Jack Gordon" and "Kyle Hammond" together, as well as news and image searches. I even searched for links between them in the databases I had access to as a licensed private investigator.

Surprisingly, all my searches came up empty.

Bored and restless from sitting in front of my computer for the last few hours, I decided to make the ninety-minute drive up to Hanover to see what I could learn at Dartmouth College.

* * *

If you asked a movie set designer to come up with the concept for a quintessential college campus, chances are good they'd create something that looks like the main Dartmouth Green.

A rectangular space more than five acres in size, the Green serves as Dartmouth's aesthetic focal point and campus social center. During homecoming each fall, the freshman class builds a bonfire on the Green. In the winter, you can find giant snow sculptures there.

Crisscrossed by seven unpaved footpaths, the Green is surrounded on all sides by college buildings of different styles and periods. But the campus's iconic image is formed by the structure on the north side of the quad, Berry-Baker Library, and its Baker Tower—which is modeled after Philadelphia's Independence Hall.

I parked in a garage two blocks south of the Green and walked around the corner to the administrative building where the school's Office of Communications was located.

I had called ahead before leaving my hotel room, and a young man named Greg Choi was waiting for me. He greeted me with a friendly smile and a handshake, and he walked me across the

Green to Webster Hall, a building just in front of Berry-Baker Library that houses the Rauner Special Collections Library and the college's archives.

Choi introduced me to an assistant archivist named Melanie Downs. She wore oversized glasses; large, loopy earrings; and a long, flowing skirt.

With sparkling eyes and an effervescent smile, Melanie showed me where I could find photographs and other records from fraternity gatherings on campus, as well as football game tailgates and other college events.

I spent the next few hours bent over stacks of pictures and other records, looking for confirmation that Gordon and Hammond had spent time together after graduating from college. The only such artifact I could find was a picture of the two of them with their arms around each other from an Alpha Chi Alpha football tailgate some ten years earlier.

Although I took a picture of the photograph with my phone, I had to admit it was hardly the compelling piece of evidence I was looking for.

As I realized I wasn't going to find anything useful, I closed the binders on the table in front of me with a sigh. I thanked Melanie for her help and left the library.

After a brief stroll around the Dartmouth campus to stretch my legs, I ended up at Molly's, a popular college hangout a few blocks from where I had parked. Since it was now early evening, I headed inside for dinner.

The restaurant looked like you might expect a campus hangout to look, with booths constructed of dark wood and college paraphernalia lining the walls: footballs from major gridiron victories, a photo of John Belushi wearing a Dartmouth sweater. (One of the writers of *Animal House* was said to have been inspired by his experiences in Dartmouth's Alpha Delta Phi fraternity.)

After the day's futility, I wanted nothing more than to comfort myself with a giant plate of nachos and an ice cold beer. Instead, I remained disciplined, ordering a sesame ginger salad and an unsweetened iced tea.

While I ate my salad, I thought about how strange it was that Hammond—a guy who craved the spotlight and sought publicity wherever he could get it—couldn't be found in any recent photos with Gordon.

Similarly, wouldn't Gordon want to showcase the state's contract with Tree Kings as a success story that had unique appeal to both sides of the political spectrum? The outsourcing of a public service to a private, for-profit entity who could deliver this service more efficiently was every conservative's dream, while managing public lands in an environmentally responsible (and climate-friendly) way would seem to make progressives happy.

It was like the two men had gone out of their way to keep their association a secret.

Connor's suggestion that Hammond didn't want to call attention to his relationship with Gordon made sense on one level, especially if there was any question about the legitimacy of the bidding process. But still, it seemed noteworthy that I couldn't find *any* public acknowledgment that they knew each other at all.

And certainly not from a lack of trying.

* * *

On the way back from Hanover, I took a short detour through

my neighborhood to see if I could spot my attackers again before returning to my hotel.

This time, I got lucky.

Parked half a block down from my apartment building was a blue Chevy Camaro, its front seat occupied by two shadowy figures.

At least the day wasn't a total failure.

Although the attempt on my life was technically being investigated by the Manchester Police Department, I had no doubt it was connected with the break-in at Callie's apartment and with the crash that killed Mark and Maggie in Concord. As a result of my meeting with Detective Connor earlier that morning, Connor knew about all of these events and how I thought they were related.

I called Connor and got his voice mail. I left the license plate number of the Camaro and a description of the car.

"If you can get a unit here soon, you can pick them up tonight," I said. "But be careful. At least one of them is armed."

* * *

Continuing their West Coast road trip, the Red Sox opened a three-game series in Oakland that night. The score was tied at one apiece when I got a call from Connor around eleven p.m.

"We have one of your boys in custody. The other one got away. Want to come talk to him?"

"You bet!" I exclaimed. "I'll be there in half an hour."

Chapter 9

When I got to the Concord police station, Connor filled me in on what happened. He'd called the Manchester PD and coordinated the arrest after listening to my message. Connor and his partner had taken the lead, and they were backed by a two-person unit from Manchester.

Connor and his partner, Detective Marco Bernardi, pulled up behind the Camaro in an unmarked car and flashed their lights. The two Manchester police officers approached from the opposite end of the block.

The Camaro took off and accelerated up the street. The Manchester cruiser blocked the road, forcing the Camaro to swerve into a lamppost. The passenger-side occupant bailed out of the car, fired off a few rounds at the Manchester unit, and disappeared down a side alley. The Manchester cops chased him on foot but soon lost contact.

The driver of the Camaro was stunned by the collision. Connor and Bernardi were able to pull him from the car and cuff him without incident.

"The Camaro was registered to the driver," said Connor as he chewed on a banana-flavored piece of Laffy Taffy. "His name's Gary Boudreau. Born upstate, lives in Concord now. Has a long list of priors. Mostly small-time stuff, like hotwiring cars and taking them for joyrides when he was younger. But he also did a three-year stretch up in Berlin for assault." Berlin was where the New Hampshire State Prison for men was located.

Connor led me into the interrogation room where Boudreau was being held.

Boudreau was a colossus of a man in his early thirties, though his face had aged prematurely—probably from hard living. I had been so focused on the guy with the gun when I'd been hiding in my closet that I hadn't noticed how large his partner was.

Because it was dark and my attackers had been wearing ski masks, it was impossible for me to tell for sure whether this was him. But the look of surprised recognition on Boudreau's face when I walked in was a compelling sign.

"That's him," I lied to Connor. "That's the guy I saw in my apartment Friday night."

"You can't know that!" he cried out.

"Why not?" Connor said.

"Because I was—" He stopped himself just in time. "Because I was never there."

So close. He had almost admitted his guilt by insisting he'd worn a mask.

Boudreau didn't seem very bright, but sometimes experience is a good substitute for intelligence. He'd evidently had a lot of experience in talking to the police before, and it had saved him there.

I watched as Connor questioned Boudreau for another few minutes, but it was a waste of time. Boudreau had nothing further to say.

As Boudreau was being led to a holding cell, Connor took

me aside. He knew my identification of Boudreau had only been a ploy to get Boudreau to admit his guilt, as I'd told him before that the two men had worn ski masks.

"We've got him on trying to run when we picked him up, but that's it at the moment," Connor said. "He'll be out in seventy-two hours unless we can find something else to charge him with."

Something Connor had mentioned earlier got me thinking. "You'd said Boudreau has experience hotwiring vehicles. The dump truck that rammed Mark and Maggie was reported stolen. Maybe he was the driver."

"We've been pulling security camera footage from the area near the collision. I'll see if we can match any of the images we might have of the truck's driver to Boudreau."

***

It was after one o'clock in the morning when I got back to my hotel room.

The Red Sox had stopped their two-game slide by beating the Athletics, 8-3. I watched some of the postgame coverage, then flipped over to a *Friends* rerun. It was the one where something funny happened to one of the friends, and then Chandler made some jokes.

After everything that had happened in the past week, I was having trouble sleeping at night. I was burning the midnight oil thinking about this case, and I wasn't getting nearly enough REM sleep.

Although I was disappointed that I hadn't made any headway in establishing a connection between Gordon and Hammond, I was buoyed by the capture of one of my attackers earlier that evening. If Connor could find video footage tying him to the murders of Mark and Maggie, then maybe he'd give up his employer to avoid facing a lifetime in prison. It might be just the break in the case we needed.

It was well into the night when I finally managed to catch some Zs. But I'd fallen asleep with the TV on. I woke up early to the sound of an excited pitchman shouting at the audience in a five a.m. infomercial.

Realizing that sleep was hopeless at that point, I got dressed and went for a drive.

The roads were quiet at that early hour, the sun still peaking above the horizon and bathing everything in a golden glow.

I took Route 101 west from Manchester, then continued straight onto Route 114 through Goffstown and past the scenic Glen Lake. At the intersection with Route 13, I turned left onto Route 13 south and followed the road along the Piscataquog River as it meandered through the tiny town of New Boston. I stayed on Route 13 through Mont Vernon and coasted down the hill toward Milford, taking in the picturesque scenery as I descended the hill.

In the quaint town center of Milford, I drove around the triangular-shaped green and continued on Route 13 south. Meeting up with Route 101 again, I turned left onto Route 101 heading back east, passing the LaBelle Winery and the Bedford Village Inn before returning to the hotel.

For the third morning in a row, I walked next door to the all-night diner and ordered breakfast, this time changing things up by requesting smoked salmon on a plain bagel with cream cheese.

Six months removed from heart surgery, I really missed getting breakfast from Dunkin Donuts.

When I got back to my hotel room, I opened my laptop and checked my email. There was a message from the state Department of Administrative Services that had been sent late the previous afternoon. I was energized to see that it was a response to my initial public records requests.

The email contained information about the internal investigation that Gordon's administration had conducted into the awarding of the state contract to Tree Kings. The message noted that the rest of the information I'd requested would follow in a separate email on Wednesday.

My excitement at seeing the subject line dissipated, however, as I scanned the contents of the attached folder. It contained very little information that I didn't already know from reading the notes on Maggie's story.

The problem with public records requests is that you're at the mercy of the civil servants you're querying. There's really no way of knowing for sure whether you're getting all the information they have—or whether some documents have strategically been omitted.

In this case, there was hardly any communication between the parties involved in the investigation, just the standard brief messages you'd expect: confirmations of interview times, summaries of findings.

If there were any further (and more revealing) exchanges, they were either not turned over—or perhaps carried out in person or through private back channels.

It was after nine o'clock in the morning when I finished reading through all of the information. Finally, those lucky souls who held normal, nine-to-five jobs had begun their work day. I decided it was time to talk with Lachlan Donovan, the losing bidder, to get his side of the story.

* * *

Donovan's company was based in Plymouth, New Hampshire, about an hour north of Manchester.

I suppose I could have arranged an online video call, but I liked to be in the room with the person I was interviewing whenever possible. You don't always notice the "tells," or giveaways when someone is lying, when you only see them from the neck up—such as fiddling with their hands or shuffling their feet.

I spoke with Donovan's executive assistant on the phone. When she learned the reason for my call, she told me Donovan was out working in the field that morning but would be more than happy to talk. She said she'd check on his availability and would get back to me right away.

Ninety seconds later, my phone rang.

"Mr. Donovan is working in Bristol today, but he says he can meet you at a coffee shop on Route 3A in Bristol at eleven o'clock. Will that work?"

"That would be great, thank you."

When I arrived at the coffee shop in downtown Bristol, Donovan was already waiting for me in a booth near the back of the restaurant. He was a towering, Bunyanesque figure with wavy red hair and a bushy orange beard. Although it was early June and the temperature was unseasonably warm, he was dressed in a scotch plaid flannel shirt, blue jeans, and suspenders. He rose to greet me amiably, enveloping my hand within his own beefy grasp.

"Thanks for meetin' me out here," he said with a hint of a lilting Irish accent. "I was just in the woods a few miles from here, puttin' together a bid for a client."

"No worries. Do you get out into the field very much?"

"Aye, as often as I can. I like to say the forest is my office."

"How long have you been doing this job?"

"I've been in this line of work for twenty years. The company itself has existed for twenty-five. It was founded by my father when we came over here from Ireland, and I've been runnin' the show for the last decade."

A waitress came over and asked if I'd like any coffee. "Just water, thanks," I replied.

Turning back to Donovan, I asked: "How big is your company, and what services do you offer?"

"We do anythin' you might need in takin' care of your forest lands. Ecological surveys, timber harvesting, silviculture, you name it. We serve public and private landowners throughout New England. We have nearly fifty employees, and last year we did close to ten million dollars in business."

"With all your experience, were you surprised to see Tree Kings win the contract to maintain the state's forests?"

"Surprised? Aye. From what I understand, cost was weighted more heavily than experience in the bidding process, and their bid came in a whisker lower than ours. When it happened a second time, I got to wondering whether the process was completely fair. The third time, we actually underbid the job quite a bit—and yet we still didn't get the contract."

After pausing to sip his coffee, he continued: "That's what really had me scratchin' my head. At the rate we quoted most recently, that contract wasn't goin' to be very lucrative. In fact, we would hardly be makin' any money. I've no idea why Tree Kings would go through the trouble of cheatin' for such a lowball figure."

* * *

When I returned to the hotel after my meeting with Donovan, I noticed the light on my room phone was blinking. Someone from the hotel's staff had called and left a message saying there was a package waiting for me at the front desk.

I walked down to retrieve the package. As I expected, it was the popup headlight assemblies for a Plymouth Superbird that I'd bought online. I checked to make sure they were in good condition. Then I called Burt and confirmed that we were all set for our meeting with Lemay later that evening.

Exhausted from not getting much sleep, I lay down on the bed and shut my eyes.

When I opened them again, the digital clock on the bedside table read 5:20. Burt was coming to pick me up in his powder-blue-and-white '57 Chevy Bel Air Sport Sedan at six o'clock. We figured Burt's car would have a much bigger impact on Lemay than my rented Ford Focus.

I hadn't thought to set the alarm, so I was lucky I woke up when I did. I took a shower to clear the cobwebs from my head while I waited for Burt to arrive.

When I saw him pull up in front of my room, I grabbed the headlight assemblies and met him in the parking lot. As I slid into the front passenger's seat, Burt seemed positively giddy at the prospect of our adventure.

"Let's go interrogate the perp!" he exclaimed.

With his silver hair and mustache, his medical background, and his enthusiasm for amateur sleuthing, he reminded me a little bit of Dr. Mark Sloan from the old TV show *Diagnosis: Murder*.

Lemay lived in a posh neighborhood in Bow, halfway

between Manchester and Concord. The houses in his neighborhood were all McMansions, four-thousand-square-foot, cookie-cutter, brick-and-vinyl homes with large bay windows and porches with cylindrical white columns. Lemay's house was the last one on the street, and it had an inground pool in the backyard.

As we pulled into the driveway, Lemay came out to greet us. He had changed from his professional attire into a tee shirt and jeans. He looked like he was in his early sixties, with wavy gray hair and a soul patch on his chin.

"Sweet ride!" he said. "Mind if I take a closer look?"

"Not at all," Burt said, popping the latch on the car's hood.

We got out of the car, and I introduced Burt as my friend. Burt lifted the front hood so Lemay could check out the engine.

"You went with the two eighty-three 4-barrel, huh?" Lemay said, looking impressed. "Cool!"

"Thanks," Burt said. "It's a little harder to tune, but I like having that extra power under the hood."

I stood back and listened to them talk shop for a few minutes. I had no idea what they were saying for much of it; I felt like I was on the Starship Enterprise, listening to Klingons talking. But Burt was doing a nice job of establishing rapport with Lemay and putting him at ease.

"So David, you're building a Plymouth Superbird?" I finally interjected. "What got you interested in that car?"

"I remember watching Richard Petty race his Superbird to eight NASCAR victories when I was growing up," he said. "I've always wanted to drive one of my own. But finding original parts for it has been a challenge. Where'd you get the headlight assemblies?"

"Oh, I picked them up at a flea market years ago," I lied. "But

I realized I'm never going to use them myself. I'm glad at least somebody will put them to good use."

"Speaking of muscle cars," Burt said, "Parker here drives a '74 Dart."

"No kidding?" Lemay said.

"Yeah. I keep meaning to restore it, but time always seems to get away from me."

"I hear that."

"This is a nice house you have," I said, changing the subject before he could ask me any questions about my car that I couldn't answer. "What do you do for work?"

"I work for the state government."

"Oh yeah? Doing what?"

"I'm actually the director of procurement for the state of New Hampshire."

"No kidding! So you oversee, like, purchasing and stuff for the entire state?"

"Yes, that's right."

"Wow, that's cool. You must have a lot of companies reaching out to you and looking to gain an edge on the bidding process. They ever offer you any money? If that was my job, I don't know if I'd be able to say no. How do you manage to stay honest? Or *do* you?"

I said it with a smile, as if we were sharing a harmless joke together, not like I was actually accusing him of anything. But he turned an interesting shade of green that I don't think I've ever seen before.

"Hey, I'm just kidding around. Sorry."

"Here," he said, reaching into his pocket, "let me give you a check for those headlight assemblies."

"They look okay to you?" Burt asked.

"Yeah, they look perfect. Thanks." Lemay seemed as if he wanted to hurry things along all of a sudden.

"Well, when you get that Superbird on the road, I'll be interested to see it," Burt said. "Maybe we'll see you at one of the local car shows?"

"Yeah, sure. See you guys around."

"What do you think?" Burt said to me as we got back into his Chevy.

"He's guilty as hell," I said. "Did you see his reaction?"

"Yup."

Lemay's response had me convinced that he was a part of whatever conspiracy was going on between Tree Kings and the state government. But just what role he played, I didn't know.

Judging from how sick he looked, I was guessing he wasn't the ringleader, but merely a pawn that others controlled.

Still, if we focused on him during the investigation, he might lead us to those in charge. And he looked like the kind of person who'd talk … if the correct pressure were applied.

Chapter 10

During Wednesday morning's cardiac rehab session, there was an animated discussion of who—if anyone—should be voted into the National Baseball Hall of Fame from the steroid era.

"Cheaters don't deserve to be rewarded, period," Mickey asserted.

"So you think anyone who tested positive for a banned substance shouldn't be eligible for the Hall of Fame?" Joe asked.

"That's right," Mickey replied.

"Then I have some bad news for you. That would mean our own beloved Big Papi shouldn't be in the Hall."

"Ortiz never officially tested positive for performance-enhancing drugs," I said, drawing on my extensive debate team experience to argue on a technicality. "It was reported anonymously that he was on a list of more than a hundred players who tested positive during survey testing by Major League Baseball before official testing began the following year. But for many reasons, league officials said the players on that list weren't necessarily taking steroids. For instance, the league said the test itself was still unreliable at that point and would often flag legal supplements."

"You may be right. But my point is, it's not as cut and dried as Mickey would like to think it is," Joe said. "Take Barry Bonds, for instance. Steroids or no steroids, he was one of the greatest players in the history of the game. How can you have a Hall of Fame that doesn't recognize your greatest players? How can you justify leaving him out as if his career had never happened?"

"Well, if that's your standard," Burt said, "then Shoeless Joe Jackson deserves to be in the Hall of Fame as well. Same goes for Pete Rose."

"Maybe they *should* be in the Hall. They're part of the history of the game."

"But doesn't the integrity of the games count for something?" I said.

"Integrity of the games?" Joe retorted. "That was already compromised as long as the league didn't have a reliable way to test for steroids. With so many players juicing back then, others took steroids just to keep up with their peers. Reliable testing cleaned up the game, but during that era, performance-enhancing drugs were the norm, not the exception. Players shouldn't be penalized for doing what they had to do to compete."

* * *

I was still thinking about this conversation as I left the hospital. If you knew others were cheating, did that make it okay to bend the rules a little yourself in order to level the playing field?

It was a question that was directly relevant to my own plans that morning, as I was about to do something that technically fell outside the law.

When I got to my car, I used my cell phone to look up the location of the nearest branch of Lemay's bank, which I knew from the check he'd given me for the headlight assemblies the previous evening. As luck would have it, there was a branch in Manchester only three miles away.

I drove to the bank, went inside, and filled out a deposit slip using Lemay's account number, which I also now possessed from the check he'd written. It's funny how stringent banks are about checking your ID when you're trying to take money *out* of an account, but not so much when you're putting money *in*.

I debated in my mind how much money I should deposit into Lemay's account, settling on a hundred dollars because it seemed like a large enough figure that my motives wouldn't be questioned. I gave the deposit slip to one of the tellers, along with five twenty-dollar bills from my wallet. For a moment I worried the teller might know what Lemay looked like, but then I realized that was unlikely in a Manchester branch.

As she handed me a receipt for the deposit, I said, "Oh yeah, I almost forgot. Could you do me a favor and print out a statement showing the recent activity in my account as well? I think I might have forgotten to record a check in my checking account register at some point."

"Sure. How far back would you like me to go, Mr. Lemay?"

"If I could see the last three months' worth of activity, that would be great."

The teller tapped a few keys on her computer, then excused herself while she walked back to the printer to retrieve the statement. She returned a few seconds later with about half a dozen printed pages and handed them to me.

"Thanks a bunch. Have a good one."

I waited to look at Lemay's bank records until I was back in my car. It didn't take me long to find something of interest.

Each month for at least the last three months, Lemay had made a nine thousand dollar deposit into his account. In cash.

"Great googly moogly!" I said out loud, though nobody else was listening.

This finding was worth the hundred dollars I had paid for it—and then some.

The amount of the deposits seemed designed specifically to avoid the automatic reporting that banks must provide to the federal government for all transactions valued at ten thousand or more. I was willing to lay odds the money was a payoff for rigging the bidding process in Tree Kings' favor.

I called Detective Connor to share my discovery.

"Do I want to know how you got this information?" he asked.

"Don't worry. I didn't hack into his bank account or anything."

"Gee, what a relief. You know I can't do anything officially with this knowledge, right? It's not admissible in court, and I can't get a warrant on the basis of this information."

"No, but you could bring Lemay in for questioning as a person of interest. Put the squeeze on him and see what happens."

"I suppose we could turn up the heat on him and see what we learn. By the way, I have some news of my own."

"Good or bad?"

"Both."

"Lay it on me."

"Who are you, Sly and the Family Stone? The good news is, we found security camera footage confirming that Boudreau was driving the dump truck that rammed your friend's car."

"That's great! *But...*"

"Even though we're charging him with two counts of second-degree murder, he still isn't talking. I'm doubtful we'll get him to give up the person who hired him. We also pulled a set of fresh prints from the passenger's side door of Boudreau's car, but they belonged to a girlfriend. We're no closer to pegging the identity of the other guy who attacked you."

*　*　*

As I drove back to my hotel, I kept thinking about what Donovan had told me the day before.

Given the modest figure Tree Kings had bid for the state forestry contract, Hammond's company wouldn't be making very much money from the deal. On the surface, it appeared that rigging the bidding process was hardly worth the hassle.

This led me to believe there was something more to the story.

But what could it be? Was Tree Kings somehow able to profit from the contract in other ways? Were they cutting down a substantially higher number of trees than they should have been felling to maintain the forest lands properly, for instance—and making a killing from the sale of this extra timber?

I seemed to have *more* questions after talking with Donovan, not fewer. That wasn't how the process was supposed to work. I felt like the investigative equivalent of an InfoWars reader: The more I learned, the less I really knew.

When I was back in my room, I called the state Division of Forests and Lands. After explaining the purpose of my call, I was connected with an administrator named Tiffany Roberts, who headed the division's Forest Management Bureau.

"Ms. Roberts, how long have you been in charge of the Forest Management Bureau?"

"It will be five years in September."

"That means you weren't in your current position when the state first awarded the contract to Tree Kings to manage its forests, right?"

"Yes, that's correct. But I was working in the bureau in another capacity, and so I'm familiar with the move to outsource the work to a private company."

"How did you feel about that decision, if you don't mind my asking? It must have been pretty controversial at the time, as I imagine it resulted in a lot of people losing their jobs."

"Well, one of the stipulations included in the contract was that the winning bidder had to hire at least two of the foresters from our division. But yes, to answer your question, it was a controversial measure, and it wasn't well received among many of our employees."

"How do you oversee the work that Tree Kings is doing, and how do you make sure the company is managing the state's forests responsibly in a way that meets your goals?"

"The Division of Forests and Lands creates a 'New Hampshire Forest Action Plan' every ten years, and this plan outlines our forest management goals and strategies. Tree Kings is tasked with carrying out these strategies. They regularly report their activities to us, and we meet monthly to discuss their progress on specific action items."

"Do you have a way to verify that they're doing what they say they will, beyond whatever assurances they give you in those meetings? For instance, is there any chance they might be cutting down more trees than they report to you, and maybe profiting from the sale of that extra timber?"

"Oh no, that can't happen. We use satellite imagery and FIA data—that is, data from the US Forest Service's Forest Inventory and Analysis program—to closely track the number of acres of forest land across the state. If that were happening, we would know about it fairly quickly."

"Would you say you're happy with the work they're doing?"

"Yes, I would say so. When they first got the contract, I had my doubts. The company hadn't been around for very long, and I was worried about their lack of experience. But I have to say that hasn't been a problem at all. From what I've seen, they've been diligent, capable, and highly responsive to our needs and concerns."

* * *

Based on my conversation with Ms. Roberts, it appeared my idea that Tree Kings might be profiting from the sale of extra timber was wrong. However, I still believed there was more to the contract that I didn't understand.

Maybe there was something else of value on the land that Tree Kings was managing, something worth killing for—like a secret vein of precious metal, perhaps?

As I was mulling over these thoughts, I called the communications office at the University of New Hampshire. I explained who I was and asked if I could speak with someone from the university's forestry department for background information on a case I was pursuing. I was hoping to learn more about the nature of the land that Tree Kings was being paid to manage for the state.

The communications department put me in touch via Zoom with a female forestry professor named, appropriately enough, Ash Duval. I assumed her full name was Ashley, but I liked the nod to a species of tree in the diminutive version of her name.

"What can you tell me about the state forest land in New Hampshire?" I asked her.

"Well, New Hampshire has just over four point seven million acres of forest land in all, and these woods support an impressive range of ecological habitats," she said. "Most of the state's trees are northern hardwoods, and the most common forest type consists of maple, beech, and birch trees. In fact, this type of timber stand makes up more than half the state's forests. White pine, red oak, and hemlock are the next most common type, followed by spruce and fir trees."

"You said there are over four point seven million acres of forest land in the state overall, and yet the state Division of Forests and Lands manages only two hundred thousand of those acres. What accounts for the rest of that land?"

"The vast majority of forest land in the state—more than seventy percent—is privately owned. Federal land, such as the White Mountains National Forest, accounts for nearly twenty percent, and the remaining ten percent is state and local public land."

"Is there anything valuable or unique about the state-owned forests? Like, could someone profit from this land in other ways besides harvesting the timber?"

"You could tap the sugar maples to make maple syrup, I suppose. But that would be illegal, and I doubt it would result in much additional income."

"You're sure there's nothing more valuable about that land? Like, maybe a vein of precious metal that no one knows about?"

She looked at me like I'd just walked into a sliding glass door.

"Well, I'm not a geologist," she said, trying not to smirk. "But I doubt there's a secret vein of gold or silver running through the state that no one else has discovered."

"Okay, thank you for your time."

As I ended the Zoom call, I thought maybe I should update the tagline on my website to read:

Parker Hanson, private investigator: Fearless enough to ask even the dumbest questions.

* * *

With all the questions I still had, it was clear I needed to learn more about Tree Kings' operation. But how could I do this when I suspected the company's owner wanted me in cold storage at the local morgue?

I couldn't infiltrate the business by applying for a job, and a direct approach was also out of the question. If I showed up on the company's doorstep again, I didn't think I would be allowed to leave alive.

I would have to learn as much as I could about the firm's activities from a distance, such as by using covert surveillance. But with an operation that large, where should I begin? Tree Kings managed more than two hundred thousand acres of forest land throughout the state. There was no way one person could observe all of that activity. It would be like trying to find Waldo amid all the artwork in Rome.

I had to come up with a plan for channeling my efforts wisely. The best way to do that was to learn as much as I could about the operation from the outside and then use this information to focus my surveillance strategically.

As I thought about how to do this, I remembered the rest of the information I'd asked for in my original Right to Know request was supposed to arrive that day. I checked my email, and sure enough, there was a message in my in-box from the state Department of Administrative Services. It included an attachment with a zipped folder containing the rest of the records I'd asked for.

Maybe there was a clue buried within this information that would point me in the right direction.

I spent the next few hours combing through all the files. They featured financial reports and descriptions of Tree Kings' activities, including copies of the written reports the company submitted to the Division of Forests and Lands each month.

The most recent of these reports indicated that Tree Kings had removed 1,247 trees from land throughout the state in the previous month, generating just over a hundred thousand dollars in income for the state.

The report also said that Tree Kings had just finished spraying forests in Sullivan and Grafton counties with an insecticide called emamectin benzoate to control for emerald ash borer and an herbicide to control for buckthorn and honeysuckle, bringing the total number of acres sprayed to a hundred and fifty thousand—with fifty thousand acres left to spray before the end of July.

In addition, I learned that the company found some tree damage during timber cruises in Carroll County, and it recommended clear cutting and planting in some stands within Coos County.

It was hardly what I'd call earth-shaking information.

In reading through the documentation, I also learned that much of the company's activity in the northern part of the state—including all of Coos County, which comprised twenty percent of the state's land—was conducted out of its Pittsburg facility. This outpost apparently had its own fuel storage unit, as there were regular fuel deliveries to that location. What's more, the box truck I'd witnessed before also made weekly supply trips to the Pittsburg location every Thursday.

After poring through all of this information, I didn't see any obvious areas for me to home in on with surveillance. Yet, I decided to start with the Pittsburg location.

I told myself this made sense because so much of the actual field work seemed to be done from this location. But maybe it was the idea that I'd be farther away from the heart of the company's operations—and Hammond's scrutiny—that attracted me.

The company's weekly supply run to Pittsburg would be taking place the next day. I could follow the truck, see what kind of routine it established, and then scope out the northern outpost at the end of its trek.

If nothing else, this gave me something active to do—and a starting point for my observation.

* * *

I had arranged with Amalia to stop by the Thirsty Moose later that evening to pick up my mail while she was tending bar. When I arrived, Kris was sitting at the bar as well. The two of them were discussing the movie they'd watched together the night before.

"Listen, I know you like Olivia Newton-John," Amalia said. "But why on Earth do you enjoy a story where the female lead transforms herself in order to be in a relationship? After seeing that movie, I've also got chills that are multiplying. But not the good kind."

"I know it seems a little dated by today's standards," Kris replied. "But the songs are catchy and the acting is great. That musical is iconic. You have to appreciate it for its time."

"Parker, help me out here," Mal said as she noticed me. "Tell Kris she has terrible taste in movies."

"I'm not wading into this argument without a drink first," I said. "Unfortunately, I'm trying to avoid alcohol."

Kris and Amalia seemed like the inspiration behind the phrase "opposites attract." And not just in terms of their taste in cinema: Whereas Mal was comfortable wearing a cutoff tee shirt, jeans, and Doc Martens, Kris had a much more highly developed fashion sense. On this night, she was wearing a coral-colored halterneck dress with a matching Coach handbag and pumps.

The conversation soon morphed from a discussion of the relative merits—or flaws—of *Grease* into a contest to see who could identify the most movie lines.

"'Hey Jakey, you've got something on your face,'" I said in a falsetto voice. "'Oh, it's a mole.'"

"That's from *Blended*," Kris said. "How about: 'I'm just a girl, standing in front of a boy, asking him to love her.'"

"That's easy," Mal said. "*Notting Hill*. I've got one: 'Three for one? How can that be profitable for Frito Lay?'"

"*Game Night*," I said. "Hey, did you know that for those overhead establishing shots of Max and Annie's neighborhood, they used a tilt-shift lens to make the actual houses look like board game pieces?"

"Where do you come up with all this information?" Amalia asked.

Good question.

If I were half as good at detective work as I was at retaining useless trivia, I might have solved the case already.

Chapter 11

I had no idea how early the truck bound for Pittsburg would be leaving from the main Tree Kings facility the next morning. To make sure I didn't miss it, I was parked across the street and down the block from the building by six in the morning. A flask of ice water and some high-protein energy bars were sitting on the passenger's seat beside me.

In my pre-surgery days, this type of early-morning assignment would call for a large French vanilla iced coffee and a sausage, egg, and cheese sandwich on a croissant from Dunkin. Instead, I'd relied on a cold shower to wake me up before I left my hotel room.

As a ritual, it wasn't nearly as enjoyable.

To pass the time as I waited, I made a mental list of my favorite TV characters of all time. I was trying to decide who should make the cut within my top five, Leslie Knope or Frasier Crane, when I saw the box truck exit the Tree Kings compound and turn left onto Route 132 heading south, away from where I was parked. The digital clock on my dashboard read 8:40.

Batter up.

I let the truck get about a quarter of a mile up the road before I pulled out and followed at a safe distance. I was lucky that the truck was beginning its journey when the sun was already well over the horizon, so the driver wouldn't notice headlights behind him.

The truck continued south under the Route 395 overpass and turned right onto Hazen Drive, toward Airport Road and the Concord Municipal Airport. Across from the airport, it turned off the road and pulled up to a small, nondescript warehouse building. A garage bay door opened, and the truck disappeared inside.

I drove past the warehouse, turned around, and parked on the side of the road a few hundred yards away, where I could see the truck when it came out again.

Standing inconspicuously within a mostly industrial landscape, the warehouse gave no outward clues as to what it might hold inside. Covered in a drab coat of peeling gray paint, the building bore the signs of weathering and neglect. There were no windows in the structure, and although it featured a loading dock whose concrete was chipped in some places, the truck had driven completely inside for some reason.

I waited nearly half an hour for the truck to reappear.

At twenty minutes past nine, the garage bay door opened and the truck emerged from the warehouse. It headed back north on Airport Road, then turned left onto Route 9 and crossed the Merrimack River.

I followed at a respectable distance as the truck turned right onto North Main Street and continued through the city, heading north on Route 3. A few miles up the road, the truck turned into the parking lot of a business called Growth Potential and circled around to the back of the building.

I pulled into the parking lot as well. Searching on my phone, I learned that Growth Potential was a distributor of professional-grade gardening, landscaping, and forestry supplies and chemicals, including herbicides and insecticides.

I went inside the building and talked with a sales associate, confirming that the loading dock for picking up supplies was located behind the building.

Then I returned to my car and waited again for the truck to emerge after securing its cargo.

Twenty minutes later, we were on the road again, headed for Route 93 north toward Pittsburg.

* * *

The traffic on Route 93 north was moderate. Again, I got lucky. It was still early in the season for there to be many people headed to the Lakes Region on a weekday, and there was just enough cover to blend in with the other cars—but not so much that I was in danger of losing my quarry.

Shortly after eleven o'clock, the box truck got off the highway in Campton. I took the off-ramp as well.

The truck turned right onto Route 49 and pulled into the parking lot of a diner just off the exit. I drove up to a gas pump across the street and watched as the driver, a tall man wearing a black-and-gold Bruins baseball cap and dressed in blue denim, got out of the cab and headed into the diner.

I waited about a minute, then drove into the diner's parking lot and risked taking a closer look. Through the diner's front window, I could see the driver sitting on a stool at the counter, looking at a menu.

I was curious about the first stop he had made at the beginning of the trip. What was the truck doing in that nondescript warehouse for half an hour, and why had it driven into the building instead of using the loading dock? Assuming it was taking on additional supplies, then what was the nature of this secret cargo? These questions had been gnawing at me since earlier that morning.

The back of the box truck wasn't visible from the diner's front window. There was no way the driver could see it from where he was sitting.

The sound I heard suddenly, echoing above the chorus to "I'm Alive" by Love and Rockets playing on my car stereo, was opportunity knocking.

On the one hand, I could continue following the truck to Tree Kings' northern outpost in Pittsburg and see if I could discover its contents by observation only. However, Hammond's operation was smart. If they had concealed the loading of the truck, chances were good they'd do the same with its unloading. I doubted I'd get close enough to see anything useful.

On the other hand, I could check the contents of the truck right now ... and with much better odds of success.

What I was contemplating was illegal. If I were caught, I could go to jail—and I would lose my private investigator's license for sure.

Perhaps I was frustrated that the investigation wasn't moving fast enough, and I was desperate for a break.

Maybe I was annoyed by the fact that two men had tried to kill me as I lay sleeping just a few nights before.

Or maybe I was tired of being haunted by the image of the burning Volvo, a disturbing reminder of how I'd tried but failed to save its two occupants from a horrible fate.

Whatever the reason, I didn't see much of a debate.

I parked on the far side of the box truck, shielded from anyone's view. I crept to the back of the truck, where I stood for a moment, alone, out of sight from the diner's patrons and from the traffic on the highway.

I figured the driver would be occupied with his lunch for at least half an hour, given how busy the diner was already that morning. I would have plenty of time to take a quick peek inside the truck, get back into my car, and park across the street again to wait for the driver to finish eating.

But first, I had to pick the lock on the cargo box door.

Fortunately, this was one of my few special talents.

I'd like to say I learned it from paramilitary training, or something else that sounds impressive. But the truth is, for the better part of my middle school years, I had aspired to be a magician on par with Harry Houdini. While other kids were working on their jump shots or tossing around a football, I would practice picking locks for hours as I imagined myself escaping from any number of submerged contraptions in front of an adoring audience.

There was no crowd to admire my handiwork that morning behind the diner. Yet, that was for the best.

Using the hole punch blade of the Swiss Army knife I carried around in my pocket, I made quick work of the padlock securing the cargo bay door. When the padlock sprung open, I unclasped the door, slid it open, and climbed into the back of the truck.

The floor of the cargo bay consisted of wooden planks, worn smooth from years of use. The walls and ceiling were made of steel. Stacked neatly against the back of the cargo bay were rows of cardboard boxes. I counted twenty stacks of boxes, each piled three high. Sixty boxes altogether.

According to their labels, the boxes all contained herbicide or insecticide for treating forest land to protect against invasive plants or pests.

None of the boxes were unmarked or bore any signs of having been loaded from the mysterious warehouse we'd stopped at initially.

To make sure the boxes contained what they said they did, I opened a few with the blade of my knife. The contents were exactly as described: plastic jugs of chemicals such as dinotefuran and emamectin benzoate.

That's odd, I thought. Maybe the truck hadn't picked up anything in that first warehouse after all. Perhaps it was dropping cargo off instead?

As I stood in the back of the truck, wondering if I had been suspicious for no reason, a sharp cry snapped me out of my reverie. *"Hey!"*

I turned around and saw a lean, hard face scowling up at me from outside the cargo bay door.

It was the truck's driver, and he looked furious.

Ruh-roh.

I had only been in the back of the truck for five minutes at most. Apparently, the driver had decided to pass on getting lunch. A Styrofoam cup of coffee was clutched in his hand.

I stepped forward and tried to look as contrite as I could while my mind scrambled for an excuse. "I'm so sorry, I was just—"

The rumble of the cargo box door slamming shut cut short my explanation, and I was plunged into darkness.

I heard the padlock snap closed, securing the door in place. A few seconds later, the engine growled to life and the truck lurched forward.

* * *

I was trapped in the back of the box truck, headed for some unknown location. Not Weirs Beach or Storyland, I was guessing.

The driver's response had stunned me. I'd assumed there would be a confrontation, and maybe he would call the police. If he'd decided to press charges, I would have found myself looking for a new career.

This was much worse.

I doubted the driver knew who I was or that Hammond presumably had ordered a hit on me already. But he was worried enough about concealing whatever illicit activity might be going on that he was willing to take some random stranger captive without even asking questions first.

He was probably on the phone to Hammond at that very moment, describing what had happened. I didn't have to think too hard to imagine Hammond's response.

You don't kidnap someone and then just let them go.

The silver lining to my situation was that the driver's actions confirmed my suspicions about Tree Kings' operations. It seemed I was right in assuming there was something shady about Hammond's forestry company, beyond the fraud that had landed him the state contract in the first place. I wouldn't have been locked in the back of the truck just for snooping around unless they had something pretty big to hide.

Unfortunately, I wasn't sure I was going to live long enough to do anything with this information—or to uncover the exact nature of the company's crimes.

There was still a small chance that I was misreading the entire situation. The Campton police station was just on the other side of Route 93, not even half a mile down the road. Perhaps the driver had locked me in the back of the truck so he could hand me over to the police in person.

However, the more likely scenario was that we were headed to Tree Kings' northern facility as planned, where the driver or someone else would dispatch me for good.

The truck turned left out of the diner's parking lot and approached Route 93. If we were headed to the police station, the truck would pass under the highway and turn left again into the parking lot of the station house.

If we were traveling north, the truck would turn right onto the highway and then accelerate.

The truck turned right, and my stomach turned along with it.

Chapter 12

If we were headed toward the Tree Kings' northern compound as I thought, then I still had a few hours to plan my escape.

Of course, it was also possible that we were meeting up with Hammond's goons at a secluded spot along the way—in which case I had even less time to come up with a solution.

Before the truck accelerated to full speed, I tried the cargo box door to see if it would budge.

As I expected, the door was locked tight.

I took out my cell phone and used the flashlight app to inspect my surroundings. The walls of the cargo box were all solid, and the ceiling looked impenetrable as well. They might as well have been made of adamantium, the indestructible metal alloy from the fictional Marvel comics.

There was nothing in the truck's cargo that could help me break out, either. No acetylene torches, crowbars, or battering rams to be found.

Too bad I hadn't continued my training as an escape artist beyond middle school.

While I was using my phone as a flashlight, I noticed to my surprise that I actually had a cellular signal from inside the truck. My brain did cartwheels as I realized: *I could call someone for help!*

If I were Spenser, I could call Hawk to arrange an ambush. If I were Easy Rawlins, I had no doubt that I could rely on Mouse to take out my captor—and he'd probably relish every minute of the process.

Unfortunately, I didn't have a kick-ass sidekick of my own.

And besides, time was of the essence. For all I knew, the driver of the box truck could pull off the highway at any moment—and I would have no idea where we were.

My best chance, and perhaps my only chance, was to call the police.

This was problematic for many reasons.

For one thing, I had committed a crime myself. I had no way of knowing how an interaction with the police would go. And I didn't enjoy the thought that I might lose my investigator's license.

What's more, I still had no idea what the nature of the criminal conspiracy involving Tree Kings was. If it somehow reached all the way to the governor's office, there was a chance the police might be an enemy, not an ally, in my current predicament.

But these were risks I felt I had to take.

I dialed 911 and told the operator I had been kidnapped. I gave her the license plate number and a description of the box truck, which by now was seared into my brain. I told her we were headed north on Route 93, just above Campton.

Then I sat down to wait, feverishly hoping the driver didn't get off at the next exit.

* * *

Not more than ten minutes later, the sound of a police siren penetrated my consciousness, and my rebuilt heart skipped a beat.

Whatever was about to happen, I immediately felt safer than I had since we left the diner. For the first time since the cargo box door had rattled shut, I felt the odds might be swinging back in my favor.

As the siren grew louder, the box truck slowed down, the driver realizing he wasn't going to outrun a police cruiser. The truck came to a stop on the side of the highway, and I braced myself for the interaction to follow.

The cargo box door rolled open, and my eyes adjusted to the bright sunshine.

"Sir, would you please step down from the back of the vehicle?"

As I jumped down, I took in huge lungfuls of air. Even though the air supply in the back of the truck was more than sufficient, being trapped inside had made it feel like my breathing was constricted.

A young state trooper stood before me. He was maybe in his mid-twenties, with a blond crew cut and a nick on his chin where he'd cut himself shaving that morning.

I scanned the officer's face for any clues as to his disposition. But his expression was blank. He would have made a good poker player.

"Sir, would you kindly turn around and place your hands behind your back?"

Before I did as I was instructed, I looked over the young trooper's shoulder. Another state trooper, this one much older, was talking to the driver of the box truck. They were standing next to the state police cruiser. The driver's hands were cuffed behind his back.

I turned around slowly, and the younger trooper handcuffed me as well. He then patted me down and removed the knife from my pocket.

"Now, would you care to tell me what's going on?"

This was the moment of truth. Or, to be more precise, the moment of untruth. What I said could determine whether I still had a job at the end of the day.

I couldn't be honest about what I was doing in the back of the truck. But I couldn't just make up any story, either. Whatever I said would be compared to the driver's version of events. If I wanted to get out of this situation without destroying my career, I had to come up with a plausible explanation that wouldn't invite more scrutiny.

My story had to align closely enough with the driver's account that it wouldn't raise any questions. Yet, I didn't know what the driver was telling the other officer. It was like navigating a narrow ridgeline in the mountains just to our north, but with a blindfold on.

I had to carefully feel my way along, and one false step could send my career plummeting.

I figured the driver would also do anything to avoid further inquiry. He wouldn't want to admit he'd locked me in the truck on purpose, so he would probably feign ignorance. If he claimed not to know I was there, then it stood to reason he wouldn't know how I got inside the truck to begin with.

I told the young trooper that I was a temporary employee working for Growth Potential and that I'd felt dizzy while loading the truck that morning. I claimed that I'd sat down for a minute behind a stack of boxes so no one would see me taking a break.

"I must have passed out or something. When I came to, I was locked in the back of the truck and we were moving. That's when I called nine-one-one."

"You told the operator you were being kidnapped. Why did you say that?"

"I don't know. When I woke up, I was confused. I'm also claustrophobic, and I guess I kind of panicked. But I realize now it was just an innocent mistake."

"You gave the operator your location. How did you know that if you'd just woken up?"

"I checked the maps app on my phone before I called. The app showed where we were."

"How did you know the license plate number of the truck?"

"Oh, uh, that's a funny coincidence. I noticed when I was loading the truck that it was the same four digits as the phone number of a girl I once dated."

"Okay, wait here." The young trooper went to confer with his partner.

My mouth was dry, my skin was clammy, and my brain was like a nearly depleted battery. I felt like I had just been through the lightning round of a high-stakes quiz show. Now, I was waiting to see the outcome.

Johnny, what do we have for our contestants today?

Well, Bob, it's a free ride in the back of a police car—and a one-night stay in a luxurious jail cell! And for lying to the authorities, we'll revoke the right to privately investigate any matters in the state of New Hampshire as a special bonus!

If the troopers did their due diligence and checked on my story, they would find out pretty quickly that I wasn't telling the truth about working for Growth Potential. I was hoping that my account matched closely enough with the driver's own version that they would let the whole thing drop and send us both on our way.

I could feel the driver's glare boring holes into my skull. I met his eyes and returned the glower, trying not to betray any fear.

As the troopers were comparing notes, their mobile radio units squawked to life. The older trooper answered his radio and had a brief exchange with the person on the other end, then disconnected and signaled to his partner to wrap things up by twirling his finger in the air.

Salvation!

The younger trooper walked back over to me and removed the handcuffs from my wrists. "We're needed on another call. We're letting you both go, but you need to be more careful from now on. I'm assuming you can catch a ride back to Concord with your trucker pal here?"

I didn't say anything, not wanting to press my luck.

I kept shifting my gaze between the troopers as they got back into their car and the trucker as he secured the cargo box door. As soon as the troopers drove away, I set off on a brisk trot toward the nearest exit, looking back over my shoulder to make sure the trucker wasn't following me.

There were enough cars on the highway to make me feel safe from the trucker once I'd put some distance between us. I watched as he climbed up into the cab, started the truck, and drove off, passing me as he continued north.

According to the map on my phone, I was about four miles from the next exit. I could have walked that distance easily enough, but it occurred to me that I wasn't safe yet. I began to worry that I might be ambushed once I got there.

I suddenly realized I no longer wanted to be alone. I'd just had my second brush with death in less than a week. I felt scared, tired, and very much exposed as I walked along the side of the highway by myself. Although the temperature was close to eighty degrees, I found myself shivering almost uncontrollably.

It was a little after noon. Because my neighbor Amalia worked nights, I thought she might be home at that hour. I called her cell phone, and she answered right away.

I explained my situation and asked if she might give me a ride back to my car.

"Of course I can come get you. I'll be there as soon as I can."

***

When Mal dropped me off at my car nearly ninety minutes later, my first instinct was to drive back to my hotel in Manchester and take a long, hot shower.

Realizing I was at the foot of the White Mountains, however, I changed my mind and decided to take advantage of my location with a brief hike instead.

Hiking was a key form of therapy for me. I often found that I was able to relax, decompress, and think more clearly after a walk in the woods. And never had I needed all of those things more than at that moment.

I kept a pair of hiking shoes and a day pack with basic hiking essentials—first aid kit, canteen, head lamp, compass, matches, rain poncho, and a lightweight tarp—in the trunk of my car. However, since my car was currently stashed at the Manchester Airport and I was using a rental, I would have to choose a short, fairly easy hike that wouldn't require any special gear, beyond the cross trainers I was currently wearing.

I popped into the diner for a Cobb salad and a tall glass of tomato juice before getting on the road. Then I drove up to Lincoln and took the Kancamagus Highway over to Albany, New Hampshire.

I got off the Kanc at Passaconaway Road and parked by the covered bridge. I stuffed the energy bars I had brought that morning into my pockets, grabbed the flask of water, and set off on the three-mile Boulder Loop Trail.

Where the trail forked, I kept to the left in order to hike the loop clockwise. Although it's only a modest elevation gain of about a thousand feet, there are some fairly steep sections of the trail. As I scrambled up the rocks, I found myself having to stop frequently to let my heart rate slow down.

When I reached the spur trail for the Ledges, I took the short detour and was rewarded with a stunning view of the White Mountains. I sat down on a ledge to rest and reflect on what I'd experienced that morning—and what it meant in the larger context of the case.

Hammond and his partners in crime would go to great lengths to preserve their secrets, including murder. They'd already proven that by killing Mark and Maggie for poking around and by attempting to take my life twice now as well.

But just what was the nature of those secrets?

With the help of certain people within the state government, Hammond's company had secured a state contract under highly suspicious circumstances—even though the total value of the contract didn't amount to very much. That suggested there was something more to the whole enterprise than just the contract itself, maybe something that having the contract facilitated.

In following the company's box truck as it made its weekly

supply run to Tree Kings' northern outpost in Pittsburg, my curiosity was piqued when the truck disappeared into an unmarked warehouse at the outset of the trip. I'd taken a shot in the dark by poking around in the back of the truck to see what I could learn. Apparently, my shot had hit its mark, as the driver's response to catching me snooping around seemed to indicate there was something highly sensitive they were hiding.

Yet, when I'd taken a glimpse inside the truck, I didn't see anything suspicious at all. All of the cargo I'd observed seemed to be innocuous. Everything appeared to be above board.

The whole thing made about as much sense as Bruce Springsteen never having a number-one hit single on the Billboard charts, despite selling more than a hundred and fifty million albums in his career.

So, what was I missing?

As I chewed on a raspberry-flavored energy bar and took in the view of the surrounding mountains, two words from this mental summary kept bouncing around inside my head.

Above board...

The answer hit me like a blindside block from a three-hundred-pound pulling guard.

Suddenly, I had a theory I wanted to verify. I was so excited that I was back at my car almost before I even realized I had started my descent.

I would have to wait another whole week before testing my theory, a length of time that was sure to seem like an eternity.

On the other hand, all that extra time might prove useful after all, as I realized I might need every minute to figure out how I was going to pull it off.

Chapter 13

After our cardiac rehab session ended the next morning, I sought out Mickey. "Got a minute to talk?" I asked him as we rode the elevator down to the hospital lobby together.

"Sure. What's up?"

I told Mickey I was looking for a small, unobtrusive camera for some surveillance work I would be doing.

"It has to be something that would easily be overlooked. And if it were magnetic, so it could be attached to a metal surface, that would be perfect."

"Oh, yeah, that's no problem. You should see some of the stuff they're coming out with these days. There are consumer-grade cameras hidden in pens, picture frames, even the bridge of a pair of glasses. Here," he said, taking an old business card from his wallet, "go to this address and ask for a guy named Dwayne. He'll set you up with whatever you might need."

* * *

Later that morning, I was standing in the electronics store that Mickey had directed me to in Nashua, listening to a tall man dressed in a purple silk shirt, gray dress pants, and black loafers talk about how the government has been covering up conclusive evidence of alien life forms on Earth.

They say it takes a village to raise a child, and that was turning out to be true of my investigation as well. So far during the course of my inquiries, I'd relied on the help of Maggie, who'd done some of the initial sleuthing before she had been killed; Jason, the *Herald's* IT director, who'd given me access to Maggie's story files and notes; Burt, who'd helped me establish a pretense for talking to the state's director of procurement, David Lemay; Detective Connor of the Concord police force, of course; and now Mickey and his former colleague in the electronics sales industry, Dwayne.

But if it takes a village to investigate a far-reaching criminal conspiracy, then Dwayne was no doubt the village idiot.

I had made the mistake of mentioning to Dwayne that I needed a surveillance camera for a case I was working on that included the possible involvement of state government officials.

"You can't trust the government, that's for sure," he was telling me. "Did you know the feds have been lyin' to us about the existence of extraterrestrials for more than seventy-five years? They did an autopsy on the aliens that crashed at Roswell in 1947. They even captured one of 'em alive, but they don't want us to know about it. I was readin' a Reddit thread the other day, and someone pointed out that you can rearrange the letters in the phrase 'Roswell alien lives' to spell out 'evil Orwellian lies.' That *can't* just be a coincidence."

I thought about what he said for a few seconds.

"But … wouldn't you need another 'S'?"

Undeterred, he continued: "The government don't want us to know they're studyin' alien technology. Now, why do you think that is? Personally, I think it's so they can keep us under their control. And once they can replicate the aliens' technology, there won't be anythin' we can do about it."

"That's fascinating," I said, "but I'm not looking to confirm the existence of aliens. I just need a simple remote camera that can transmit a live video feed over a cellular connection."

I explained that I was looking for something small that could be stuck to the inside of a truck's cargo box with a magnet, ideally painted light gray so that it would blend in with the metal wall. Dwayne told me they didn't have anything like that in stock, but he could order something or have it made. I told him it was a rush job and that I was willing to pay extra if I could pick it up within a few days.

"Sure, but a request like that won't be ready 'til Tuesday at the earliest."

The deal secured, I handed Dwayne my credit card.

"*Thanksh, Q,*" I said, doing my best Sean Connery-as-James Bond impersonation.

"Oh, have you taken the red pill, too?" he replied, leaning in closer and dropping his voice. "I suppose you know I ain't QAnon, but I guess that would be a good cover for him, sellin' electronic devices in a retail store in New Hampshire. Anyway, I hope you expose the Deep State conspiracy. Where we go one, we go all!"

Guesh he didn't get the referensh.

* * *

Having ordered a special surveillance camera from Dwayne, I was one step closer to learning why the driver of the box truck had gone to such great lengths to preserve whatever secrets

125

his employer was hiding.

I'd assumed those secrets might have something to do with the truck's cargo. But when I looked through the boxes the truck was carrying, I didn't notice anything suspicious.

Yet, what if the truck was transporting hidden contraband in a secret compartment? Say, *under the floorboards*? That would explain why the driver had reacted the way he did when he caught me snooping around.

To confirm my theory, I would have to watch the truck being unloaded. I didn't think I would be able to do this by observation alone, as it was highly unlikely to happen out in the open. That's where the video camera came in.

However, I still had to figure out a way to get the device into the back of the truck without anyone from the company knowing about it.

The main Tree Kings facility was heavily protected with a barbed-wire fence and an array of security cameras of its own. I doubted I could just sneak onto the property and plant the camera in the back of the truck myself.

For now, this was a question I still needed to think about. In the meantime, I decided to turn my attention to learning more about the mysterious warehouse the truck had disappeared into shortly after starting its trip.

I looked at an online map to identify the street address of the warehouse. Then, I searched for the property owner or business name associated with this address. The only information I could find was a limited liability company called Minerva Enterprises.

I rummaged through all the public information databases I had access to, but I couldn't gather any additional insight into who owned the company or what its purpose was. If the company had a website, I could have used the public "WHOIS" database service to find out who registered the site's domain name, but unfortunately there was no website associated with Minerva Enterprises, either.

It looked like someone had gone through a great deal of trouble to hide the company's ownership. Minerva Enterprises was most likely a shell company formed to conceal its true nature.

I didn't have the means to dig any further. But maybe Joe, the retired accountant from my cardiac rehab group, would know what to do. I found Joe's telephone number in an online directory and gave him a call.

I explained to Joe what I was looking to accomplish. He said he didn't have the tools or the know-how to learn anything more about the company behind the mysterious warehouse, either—but perhaps a forensic accountant could help.

"There's a woman I used to work with who specializes in this kind of job," Joe said. "Her name is Katherine Graham, but everyone calls her Tillie."

"Tillie Graham?" I asked incredulously.

"Hey, at least she doesn't work for Western Union."

Joe promised to call Tillie and ask her to get in touch with me. Barely an hour later, my phone rang.

"Hi Parker, this is Tillie. Our mutual friend Joe gave me your number. How can I help?"

I told her about the warehouse whose ownership I was looking to pin down. I described the steps I'd taken myself and noted that the only information I could find was a company that seemed to exist only on paper.

"Yes, that sounds like a shell company all right."

"Is that something you can help me trace?"

"Sure. Send me an email with the details, and I'll see what I can find out."

While I was emailing Tillie with the information she needed for her search, I saw that I had a message from the state Department of Administrative Services. It was a response to my additional Right to Know request for the records of everyone who had visited the governor's office in the last three years.

I had almost forgotten that I'd made this additional request. The list of visitors to Gordon's office was seven pages long. I scanned the list, but I didn't see Hammond's name—or anyone else from Tree Kings, for that matter. No other names on the list looked important to the case, either.

Another dead end.

* * *

The Red Sox were beginning a twelve-game home stand against Texas, Minnesota, Chicago, and Kansas City that evening. But they had been losing starters to injuries all season. They were down to just four regular players in the starting lineup, and the replacements hadn't been doing so well.

The game started off in promising fashion, with the Sox scoring on a double off the wall in the bottom of the first inning to take a 2-0 lead. Yet, that was the last time they would hit the ball into the outfield all night.

Ranger fans got the last laugh as Texas won the opener, 7-2.

I was watching the postgame wrap-up when my phone rang. It was Connor.

"Lemay's dead," he said abruptly, and I felt my body go numb. "He was found asphyxiated in his garage earlier this evening."

Chapter 14

"Lemay lived alone," Connor explained. "But when he didn't show up to work this morning, and his assistant hadn't heard from him all day, she called the police around four p.m. to request a wellness check. The patrolmen found him sitting at the wheel of his Mustang in the garage, unresponsive. The gas tank was empty and the garage door was closed. There were still traces of carbon monoxide in the garage. We assume the car had been running until it ran out of gas."

"Was it a suicide—or murder?"

"Hard to say. There were no immediate signs of foul play, but no suicide note, either. We'd brought him in for questioning yesterday. He seemed nervous but denied any wrongdoing in awarding the state contract to Hammond's company. When we asked him about the large monthly cash payments you said he'd been depositing into his personal checking account each month, he told us he had a rich aunt who was distributing her estate before she passed on. We hadn't had a chance to check on his story yet."

"Maybe he was worried you'd poke holes in his story, and he didn't want to face up to the consequences. Or maybe the people he was working for found out you'd brought him in for questioning, and they wanted to make sure he didn't talk."

"That's how we figure it, too. Either way, he won't be any help to us now."

***

Lemay's death was a huge blow to the investigation. I thought he might be the key to unlocking the entire case. Now that Lemay was no longer in the picture, our focus would have to shift elsewhere.

With Tillie probing the nature of the mysterious warehouse, I spent almost the entire weekend listening to deep cuts from Duran Duran while I tried to figure out how to sneak the camera I'd ordered from Dwayne into the back of the box truck.

After a great deal of deliberation, I realized two things.

The first was that John Taylor was criminally underrated as a bassist.

The second was that I needed an inside accomplice—someone who had access to the truck during the course of their job and who could plant the camera inside.

I was leery of teaming up with a Tree Kings employee unless I could target someone who seemed to be dissatisfied with the company. However, after several hours of searching through the social media feeds of everyone I could find who worked for Tree Kings, I hadn't come across a single post suggesting that anyone was unhappy with their job. All the employees I'd managed to identify seemed thoroughly gruntled.

Either Hammond kept his employees happy, or they were smart enough not to air their grievances for the entire world to see.

Plan B was to recruit an employee who worked for Growth Potential and who might have access to the Tree Kings' box truck while it was being loaded with supplies for its weekly trip to Pittsburg.

Again, I compiled a list of employees using publicly available workforce information. Then, I meticulously combed through each person's social media accounts and through public records databases to identify promising candidates. I had two main criteria in mind: workers whose information suggested they were in need of quick cash and employees with a criminal record.

After another few hours of working on my laptop, my neck ached and my brain felt like it wanted to crawl out of my skull and hitch a ride to a beach somewhere in Mexico. But I'd found two potential co-conspirators.

One was a guy from Pembroke named Lenny Kowalski whose wife had recently left him. According to Craigslist, Kowalski was looking to sell his seventeen-foot bass fishing boat so he wouldn't go into debt. The other prospect was an ex-con named John Rizzo who'd done some time for burglary.

After tracking down their phone numbers in an online registry, I reached out to Lenny first.

"Hello, Mr. Kowalski?"

"If you're selling anything, I'm not interested."

"Actually, I'm hoping you can help me—and I'm willing to pay you for your efforts."

"I wouldn't have to do anything illegal, would I?"

"Why don't I explain to you what I have in mind, and then you can tell me what you think."

I told Kowalski I was a private investigator who suspected one of the companies that purchased supplies from his employer of illegal activity, but I couldn't prove it without seeing the truck being unloaded. The only way to do that was to sneak a camera into the back of the truck. (I left out the fact that New Hampshire law prohibits non-consensual video surveillance within any private area.)

"I have a tiny video camera that attaches to the inside wall of the truck with a magnet," I continued. "All you would have to do is attach the camera while you're loading the truck on Thursday. For this simple act, I'm willing to pay you five hundred dollars—half when I give you the camera and half when the job is done."

"Mmmmm, I don't think so. I can't afford to lose my job if I get caught."

"You're sure I can't change your mind? Five hundred dollars is a lot of money."

"No. I wouldn't be comfortable doing that. But good luck finding another option."

At that point, my only other option was Rizzo. So, I gave him a call.

"Mr. Rizzo? My name is…"

"Sorry, pal. Wrong number."

"John, wait—what if I told you I have a really easy job in mind for you, and for just thirty seconds of your time I'm willing to pay you five hundred dollars?"

That got his attention.

I told Rizzo what I was looking to accomplish, but this time I left out my motives. I didn't think he needed to know who I was or why I was looking to spy on Tree Kings' activities.

Rizzo said he would accept the assignment. We agreed to the same terms I'd offered Kowalski, and I told him I'd meet him outside the Growth Potential facility to hand over the camera when his shift got over at six p.m. on Tuesday.

* * *

When Callie and I were having dinner the week before, she told me that her studio's annual dance recital was that weekend. On Sunday evening, I called her to find out how the recital had gone.

"It went well, thanks for asking," she said. "No one fell and broke a leg, so I'd say it was quite a success."

"And how are you coping with Maggie's passing? Are you doing okay?"

"Yeah, I suppose. Some days are better than others. My sister has been very helpful. But I still feel a tremendous sense of loss."

"If there's anything I can do, let me know."

"Thanks. Actually, would you like to get together again sometime? Now that dance is over for the summer, I have a lot of time on my hands. But I don't want to be alone too much with my thoughts, and I think my sister could use a break from me as well."

"Yes, of course. I'd like that."

We agreed to meet up again that Wednesday. Because she'd invited me to the Capitol Center performance the previous weekend, I volunteered to plan our next outing.

I was feeling pretty good about the way things were shaping up that night. I'd talked with Callie, and we were going to see each other again later that week. I'd also figured out a way to discover what was so important—and highly sensitive—about the supplies that Tree Kings was transporting to its facility in the northern part of the state each week. I had a strong gut feeling that obtaining this information would go a long way toward cracking the case and getting justice for Mark and Maggie.

Lemay's unfortunate demise on Friday seemed like it might derail the entire investigation. Some forty-eight hours later, however, it appeared my luck might be changing.

All things considered, it had turned out to be a fairly successful weekend.

With Boudreau in jail, I suppose I could have moved back into my apartment. But I was keenly aware that his associate—the one who carried a handgun equipped with a silencer—remained on the loose, and I didn't want to risk making it easier for him to find me. So, I was still holed up at the Holiday Inn near the airport.

Yet, living in a hotel room made it harder to eat well. I couldn't just make my own meals, and I was getting tired of eating out and trying to choose healthy foods from the rather limited menus that most establishments offered.

That evening, I solved the challenge by Doordashing a Mediterranean bowl from a local restaurant for dinner. As I waited for my food to arrive, I lost myself in an old Hitchcock film on Turner Classic Movies that I hadn't seen since college: *Dial 'M' for Murder.*

Though I hadn't handled this case nearly as deftly as Chief Inspector Hubbard solved the murder in the film, I felt like I was finally making progress—and if all went well, I was on the verge of breaking it wide open later that week.

* * *

As excited as I was on Sunday, by Monday evening my mood

had soured. I was impatient for Thursday to roll around so I could put my plan into action. There wasn't much I could do in the meantime.

Tillie was still researching the ownership of the unknown warehouse. Lemay was no longer a lead, and neither was Boudreau. I hadn't been able to connect Hammond with Gordon or other members of his administration so far, but I was out of fresh ideas on that front.

It seemed as if the entire investigation was on pause until later in the week, when Tree Kings' regular supply run to Pittsburg would happen again.

I felt like I was stuck in a snowbound cabin waiting for the roads to clear before I could go anywhere, with only a collection of dice to occupy me. There were only so many games of Yahtzee you could play before you started to go out of your mind with restlessness.

Like Tom Petty sang: *The waiting is the hardest part.*

To pass the time, I woke up before sunrise Tuesday morning. I drove to the airport and retrieved my hiking gear from the back of my Dart. I returned to my hotel room, filled my canteen with water, and put on my hiking boots. Then I drove up to the Kancamagus Highway, took the Kanc toward Albany again, and parked at the Champney Falls Trail head, not far from the Boulder Loop Trail I'd hiked the week before. I set out on the trail past the falls and toward the summit of Mount Chocorua.

Chocorua stands at the southern edge of the White Mountains. At thirty-five hundred feet in elevation, it's not one of New Hampshire's famed four-thousand-foot peaks. Yet it's one of the most frequently climbed mountains in the state, and for good reason: It offers incredible, 360-degree views from its distinctly shaped summit above the tree line, including a perfect view of the many White Mountains peaks to the north and west.

The eight-and-a-half-mile trek from the Champney Falls Trail head to the summit and back is moderately challenging, with about twenty-five hundred feet of elevation gain. Before my heart attack, I'd completed the hike with ease many times. On this occasion, though, I took it slowly and stopped to rest often, trying to keep my heart rate at a safe level.

I began my hike at six-thirty a.m. and didn't get back to the parking area until nearly three in the afternoon, giving me just enough time to pick up the video camera I'd ordered from Dwayne in Nashua and deliver it to Rizzo in Concord for six o'clock.

As I pulled out of the Champney Falls parking area, I felt triumphant. Although I'd just completed a hike I'd done many times before, scaling a mountain that barely cracked the list of the hundred tallest peaks in New Hampshire, it seemed like I'd conquered Mount Everest.

That was the most strenuous workout I'd done since my operation. Not only was I still standing, but the hike was confirmation that life as I knew it before hadn't ended after my surgery.

The drive back to Nashua took two hours. Dwayne wasn't working at the electronics store that afternoon, but another sales associate gave me the camera I'd ordered. I thanked her and headed up to Concord.

When I pulled into the Growth Potential parking lot, Rizzo was already waiting for me. He was a thick, heavy-set man of an indeterminate age: He could have been anywhere from twenty-five to forty-five years old. He had short, dark hair, and a scruffy beard tried but failed to cover his flushed cheeks.

"You Hanson?" he said as I approached.

"Guilty as charged."

"Now, that's a phrase I ain't ever said before."

I handed him the miniature camera along with two hundred fifty dollars in cash. I showed him how to turn it on and how to attach it to the inside of the truck as it was being loaded.

"Thanks for helping me out, John," I said. "I really appreciate it. I'll come by again on Friday afternoon with the other half of your money."

"Sure, no problem. Nice doing business with you."

* * *

The Red Sox were taking on the Twins at Fenway Park Tuesday night. They'd lost the series with the Rangers over the weekend and were in danger of dropping out of contention in the American League East before the All-Star break.

The Minnesota series didn't start on a positive note, either. The Sox squandered a terrific pitching performance from their starter and middle relievers by failing to score any runs for themselves. The game was decided in the top of the ninth inning with a moon shot into the Green Monster seats by a minor league callup I'd never heard of named Billy Thompson.

Twins 2, Red Sox 0.

Though the game was disappointing, I didn't mind. In fact, I went to bed feeling much better than I'd felt the night before.

After all, I was seeing Callie the next day.

And the day after that was finally "go time." With the camera now in Rizzo's hands, I was soon going to learn what the driver of the box truck had been so anxious to hide.

Chapter 15

I told Callie I would pick her up for our second outing at her sister Clio's house in Derry, where she had been staying since the break-in at her apartment. She was reluctant to return to her own residence in Concord until the criminals responsible for Maggie's death had been caught.

I understood completely. In fact, I was in the same position. I felt better about Callie's safety knowing that she wasn't alone in her apartment. In the meantime, she and I were both exiles from our homes, living in limbo until the case was finally resolved.

I pulled up to Callie's sister's house just after five o'clock on Wednesday evening.

Clio and her husband Bill lived in a quiet neighborhood consisting of two-story colonial houses with fenced-in yards. Theirs was a light gray house with white trim, black shutters, and a black front door with a brass knocker.

Callie emerged from the house and skipped down the front steps to greet me. She wore a spaghetti strap top, khaki shorts, and sandals. She was carrying a lightweight button-down shirt in case the weather turned chilly.

"Where are we going?" she asked as she slid into the car beside me.

"Well, you shared your biggest passion with me the last time we were together, so I figured I would do the same with you tonight."

"Great! So ... we're going to investigate someone?"

"Hey, I'm a complex person with many interests. For instance, do you like baseball?"

"You mean the sport where you run around in knickers and try to hit a little white ball with stitches on it?"

"Well, there's a lot more to it than that. But yes."

"I'm just teasing you. Yes, I like baseball. In fact, my dad was a third baseman for Northeastern during his college years. He took my sister and me to a lot of games when we were growing up."

"That's cool. I thought we might catch a New Hampshire Fisher Cats game tonight. But first, what do you say we get something to eat?"

* * *

Before heading to the game, we stopped at the Food Truck Park on Willow Street in Manchester for an early dinner.

"Do you like tacos?" I asked.

"Doesn't everybody?"

"This guy I know, Ray Johnson, makes the best tacos in the city."

We approached Ray's taco truck and read through the specials on the menu board as he finished serving another customer.

"Hey, Ray."

"Parker, my man, what's going down?"

"Information literacy. Trust in our public institutions. The balance on my retirement account."

"I hear that."

"Ray, I'd like you to meet my friend Callie."

"It's nice to meet you," Ray said, shaking Callie's hand. "Any friend of Parker's is a friend of mine."

"How do you two know each other?" Callie asked. "All those taco Tuesdays over the years?"

"Actually, Parker helped connect me with my birth mother."

"Really?"

"Yeah. My mom hired him to track me down a few years ago. She was only sixteen when she had me. She was estranged from her own parents, and she knew it would be too big of a responsibility to raise me on her own. It took her thirty years to work up the courage to look for me, and I'm so glad she did. Turns out I was living only twenty minutes away, and neither one of us had any idea."

"That's such a wonderful story."

"Yep," I said, "and now Ray gives me the friends-and-family discount on tacos."

"It's the least I can do."

"How is your mom, by the way?"

"She's doing good. I'm taking her up to Bar Harbor for the Fourth of July weekend."

Callie ordered two shrimp tacos on corn tortillas with avocado crema and cabbage slaw. I asked for two grilled tilapia tacos on corn tortillas with avocado slices, shredded cabbage, salsa verde, and pico de gallo.

"We're on our way to the Fisher Cats game," I said to Ray. "Tell your mom I said hi. And enjoy your trip. It was nice to see you again."

"Thanks, man. You, too."

As we returned to the car, Callie said, "Admit it. You brought me here just so I'd hear that story and know what a nice thing you did for Ray and his mom."

"No, really—it was all about the tacos. I swear."

"Mmmmm," she said, taking a bite. "They are pretty amazing."

* * *

The Fisher Cats were the Double A affiliate of the Toronto Blue Jays. They played at Delta Dental Stadium, a beautiful ballpark located on the Merrimack River in Manchester.

We parked in the Southern New Hampshire State University Millyard parking garage and made the short walk to the stadium next door.

"Did you ever play baseball yourself?" Callie asked.

"Little League when I was ten. I knew enough to give up the game when my coach said I had an arm like a leg."

"Ouch."

Our seats were in section twelve, behind the home team's dugout along the first base line. Because it was a Wednesday night and school was still in session for a few more days, the stadium was barely half full.

Callie ordered a summer ale and I got a bottle of water, and we settled into our seats.

The weather was perfect for taking in a game. The golden-hour sunlight cast the stadium in a warm glow, and a soft breeze kept the temperature comfortable. Our seats were perfect, too: We had an ideal vantage point to see all the action up close, to smell the fresh cut grass and hear the smack of the ball hitting the players' mitts.

Unfortunately, the play on the field didn't live up to the beauty of the setting, as the Fisher Cats lost an error-filled game to the Binghamton Rumble Ponies, the Double A affiliate of the New York Mets, 3-1.

In fact, the most excitement we saw on the field was the entertainment between innings, when a guy who called himself the Amazing Harris balanced various objects on his chin—including an eight-foot stepladder and even a wheelbarrow.

When the game was over, we walked to a nearby bar for another drink before heading home.

"Sorry that wasn't the best game," I said.

"That's okay," she said, displaying a lightning-quick wit. "We'll always have Harris."

If it was possible, I think I liked Callie even more at that point.

Her long, dark hair fell loosely around her shoulders. Her light gray eyes seemed both inviting and inscrutable at the same time.

I thought I could lose myself in those eyes, like staring into the embers of a campfire on a chilly autumn night.

"So, what's new with the case?" she asked.

I gave her a rundown and told her I might be on the verge of a breakthrough in the investigation the next day.

"That sounds exciting."

"It is. But most of all, I just want justice for Mark and Maggie."

Callie's face grew pale, and I cursed myself for saying Maggie's name. It was clear that Callie was still having a hard time with the death of her close friend.

To change the subject, I sought to learn more about her background. "You said your mom teaches at UNH. Did you grow up in Durham?"

"I did. I studied theater and dance at Bowdoin, and after college I moved to New York City to try to make it on Broadway."

"Did you have any luck?"

"I was in the ensemble for a few shows. But after three expensive years of mostly waiting tables, I realized I wasn't going to get steady work, and so I moved back to New Hampshire. I got a job teaching at the studio, and that's where I've been ever since."

"Were your parents disappointed that you chose dance?"

"Oh, no. On the contrary, they've been incredibly supportive. The arts were always important in our family."

"That's good to hear."

"What about you? Are you from this area originally?"

"No, I grew up in a small town in western Massachusetts called Chesterfield. My dad was an electrician, and my mom ran a small daycare business. They're both retired now. I got my bachelor's degree from UMass Boston and went to work at the newspaper right out of college."

"Do you have any siblings?"

"Just one. An older brother named Luke. He lives in Arlington, Virginia, and works for the Navy."

"Do you see him often?"

"Not really. We're not very close. You know how older brothers can be."

I regretted the words as soon as they passed through my lips.

I'd gone and done it again. Reminded Callie of another tragic loss.

I felt like a living incarnation of the meme from *The Simpsons* in which Sideshow Bob steps on one rake after another.

"I'm so sorry. That was insensitive of me."

"No, it's okay." But though her words said one thing, her body language communicated something else altogether.

Not anger or frustration with me for sticking my foot in my mouth. More like profound sadness. Her body sagged like an inflatable tube man outside a car dealership would react if someone accidentally tripped over the fan's power cord.

"Would you like me to take you home?" I asked.

"Actually, I think I'd like another glass of wine."

* * *

As Callie sipped her glass of sauvignon blanc, the song playing over the speakers in the bar was Adele's "Rolling in the Deep." It seemed like a fitting selection, as our conversation had just ventured into deeper waters.

"When my brother died a few days before his eleventh birthday, my mother just sat alone in her bedroom for days," she said. "It was my aunt who took care of my sister and me."

"We all process grief in different ways. I'm sure she did the best she could under trying circumstances."

"I know that now. But as a child, I was so angry with her. I thought she was being selfish, so wrapped up in her own sorrow that she wasn't thinking about the rest of her family. I don't want to be that paralyzed by grief myself."

"That's understandable. But it's okay to be sad—and to allow yourself the time you need to heal."

"I guess time heals all wounds, huh?"

"It *is* a wound. And time will help. But you also need more than that."

I continued: "When somebody we're close to dies, it's like

their absence tears a big chunk from our soul. All the love and light and purpose they gave us is suddenly gone. Not gone entirely, because we still have their memory. But a significant part of that life force is gone.

"To heal properly, I think we have to replenish that energy somehow. It can come from the extra love and support we feel from others, or from making a new friend or connection, or from doing some activity that nourishes our soul, or from keeping alive the memory of the person we lost. Usually, it comes from some combination of these factors. But the faster and more fully we replenish this life force, the quicker we're able to heal."

"Thank you. That's a good way of thinking about it."

"Would you like to talk about Maggie? For instance, how did the two of you meet?"

"I was looking for a place to live in Concord, and she was looking for someone to share her apartment. I'll never forget the ad she'd posted. It said: 'Roommate wanted. Nonsmoker, neat freak. Fans of good sketch comedy, bargain wines, and new cultural experiences a plus. No bigots, narcissists, or Kid Rock fans. If you've ever berated a service industry employee, please don't apply.'"

"Yeah, that was Maggie all right. She had a real way with words."

* * *

Later that evening, after bringing Callie back home to her sister's house, I walked her to the front door. The night was quiet, with only the sound of summer crickets chirping to disturb the silence.

Callie looked into my eyes for a few seconds, then wrapped her arms around my neck in a tight embrace, as if the ground had suddenly dropped beneath her feet and she was holding on for dear life.

Resting her head on my chest, she said: "Spending time with you has helped replenish me."

I squeezed her body gently in response.

"I'd invite you in," she whispered, "but I don't think that would be fair to either of us. I'm still trying to process a lot of grief, and that's something I need to do on my own. But when I'm ready, maybe we could go on an actual date?"

"I'd like that."

She let go of my neck, took my hands in hers, and said: "Right now I feel like I need you. But I'd like to wait until I only *want* you. Does that make sense?"

"Yes, it does."

She kissed me lightly on the cheek, flashed me a departing smile, and disappeared inside the house.

Chapter 16

I left Callie's sister's house with a jumble of emotions.

I was elated that Callie had feelings for me. Frustrated that our mutual attraction had to wait.

But most of all, my heart ached for the emptiness she was still feeling.

Losing her brother in an accident at such an early age must have been devastating. Losing her roommate all these years later only amplified the trauma.

I was a little jealous that she could seek solace in the comfort of alcohol. I wanted nothing more than to stop at another bar myself on the way back to my hotel and down a pitcher of beer and some wings.

The only thing preventing me was the memory of those first few weeks after my surgery, when I couldn't even push myself out of bed—and I was worried I'd never be whole again.

As I plopped down on the bed in my hotel room, I was saved from a long night of staring up at the ceiling by a single, consoling thought.

In about twelve hours' time, I would finally be learning what was so sensitive about the cargo in Hammond's truck that his driver was willing to have me killed to preserve the secret.

* * *

I slept in until eight-thirty the next morning. When I woke up, I took a quick shower, got dressed, and set up camp in front of the desk in my hotel room. My laptop was plugged in and a flask of water was within easy reach as I waited for the camera feed to go live from the back of the box truck.

As the clock in the top right corner of my computer screen advanced to nine thirty—and then 9:45—and no images had popped up, I began to panic.

What if the truck didn't stop at Growth Potential this week?

Yes, it was the busiest time of year for spraying to control the spread of destructive weeds and insects in the state's forests. But what if the supply of chemicals the company had transported to its northern outpost the week before was still sufficient for the job?

My fears proved unfounded when, a few minutes before ten o'clock, I was staring at a live feed from the camera on my computer screen.

The image was a little grainy, but there was Rizzo's pock-marked face staring back at me.

He gave me a "thumbs up" signal and disappeared from the frame. In his place, I saw stacks of boxes in the back of the truck.

We were good to go.

The image lasted for a few more seconds, and then the screen went dark again. The camera was motion sensitive, and so it was triggered by any movement that it picked up within the frame.

I waited to see if it would come on again a few minutes later, but when it didn't, I assumed the truck was fully loaded and ready to resume its trip north.

If this was the truck's last stop on its way to Pittsburg, then it might be at least three hours before the camera turned on again to reveal the truck being unloaded. However, I didn't want to stray from my computer at all, for fear of missing any unexpected images while the truck was en route.

I suppose I could have used my cell phone to watch the live video feed from wherever I was, but I didn't trust the reliability of my cellular connection. And besides, I preferred to view a larger image size so that I could see the picture in more vivid detail. So, I settled in for a long morning of waiting in front of my laptop.

To pass the time, I played vintage arcade games like *Donkey Kong* and *Galaga* on my computer using a simulator program. I also completed a few Thursday crossword puzzles from the *New York Times* archives. (Although the Friday and Saturday puzzles are harder, I preferred solving themed puzzles, and the end-of-the-week crosswords are themeless.)

At 11:44, the live video feed kicked on again, and I closed the browser window containing the puzzle I was working on. I wasn't expecting an image from the camera so soon, and I shivered with excitement.

But the camera image was very dark, as if the truck's cargo door hadn't been opened yet. From what I could make out before the image disappeared a few seconds later, there was no sign of activity inside the truck's cargo box.

False alarm. Perhaps the camera had been activated when the truck hit a bump in the road.

As the time stretched beyond noon, my stomach began to rumble. But I didn't dare leave my post in front of the laptop, even though the truck wasn't likely to arrive at its destination for another hour or so. I could have Doordashed lunch, but I didn't want any distractions pulling me away from my computer screen even for a few seconds. So I blocked out the hunger pangs from my mind and focused instead on solving the crossword clues.

As one p.m. rolled around, my anticipation grew. I found myself tapping the heel of my foot on the floor with nervous energy as I stared at the screen, waiting for something to happen.

By one fifteen, I began to worry the camera had failed.

Shouldn't the truck have arrived at its destination by now? I wondered.

By one twenty, I was having a hard time sitting still in my desk chair. I wanted to burn off the excess energy I felt by powering the truck to move faster, like a hamster running in a wheel connected to a generator.

At 1:23 p.m., the live video feed appeared again in my web browser.

Show time!

I was looking at the back of an unidentified man as he moved in front of the camera's field of vision. He grabbed a box from the top of one of the stacks, turned around, and shuffled past the camera and out of the frame. A few seconds later, I saw the truck's driver do the same thing.

This pattern of activity repeated itself for several minutes as the two men unloaded the boxes from the back of the truck. From what I could tell, all of the boxes were labeled with chemicals from Growth Potential like the ones I'd seen when I had been trapped in the back of the truck the week before.

It took nearly twenty minutes for the men to unload all of the boxes. Finally, the back of the truck was empty.

I leaned in closer to my laptop and held my breath.

Was I actually going to learn if there was a secret compartment under the floor as I'd suspected?

The driver appeared in the frame again. But instead of crouching down on the floor of the cargo box and opening up a secret compartment, he turned and looked directly into the camera.

A crooked grin spread across his face as he pressed his nose up close to the camera lens, and I could see wicked intentions glisten in his eyes.

Then he took a step back, cocked his fist, and brought it hurtling forward with tremendous force.

As his knuckles made contact with the small spy camera, the image went dark.

* * *

I sat in stunned silence for a few moments, trying to process what I'd just witnessed.

The driver's punch might as well have been aimed at my stomach, as it had the same effect of knocking the wind from my sails.

A week's worth of planning and investigation had just gone down the tubes. Not to mention the loss of a perfectly good—and fairly expensive—surveillance camera.

Even worse, I was back to square one in trying to solve the mystery of what Tree Kings was hiding. And I had no idea where to go from here.

Once I managed to regain my breath, I began to wonder: *How did the driver know the camera was there?*

If the driver or his colleague had looked directly at the

camera while they were unloading the truck, that might have indicated they'd noticed its presence. Yet, not once did that happen the whole time they were working.

Did they somehow know about the camera in advance?

I called Rizzo to ask if he knew what had happened—and just as importantly, why.

"John, did anyone see you place the camera inside that truck? Did you tell anyone what you were doing?"

There was a pause on the other end of the line.

"No, why?"

"The driver of the truck just smashed the camera to smithereens before I could see anything valuable."

"You're still gonna pay me the rest of the money you owe me, right?"

I ignored his question.

"Did you attach the camera in the corner of the truck like I told you to? It should have blended in with the metal wall of the cargo box nicely. I have no idea how the driver would have spotted it, unless he knew about it beforehand."

"Are you suggesting I had something to do with that camera being destroyed?"

"I just don't understand how it could have happened, unless he was tipped off."

Rizzo surprised me by laughing.

"Maybe you're not such a bad detective after all."

"Who told you I was a detective?"

"When you offered me five hundred dollars to stick a little camera inside the back of that truck, I wondered to myself what was so important that you were willing to fork over that kind of cash. It got me thinking that maybe the guy who owned the truck would *also* be willing to pay to keep whatever secrets he was hiding."

That sleazy bastard.

"I talked with the company's owner," Rizzo continued, "and he said you were a detective who was harassing him. He offered to pay me double if I told him what you'd hired me to do."

"You spoke with Hammond?"

His laugh pierced my gut like a stiletto. "Maybe that'll teach you never to trust someone who's a criminal."

Chapter 17

Not since the 2003 collapse of the Old Man in the Mountain—the iconic, forty-foot rock formation whose image appears on all state route signs across New Hampshire—had someone lost face this badly in the Granite State.

I felt about as good at my job as the guy who'd pitched his bosses on the idea for New Coke in the '80s.

If I didn't have a compelling reason to go to cardiac rehab the next morning, I might have just stayed in bed all day. But it was Burt's last day in the twelve-week program. I'd bought him a little heart-shaped stress ball as a gag gift, and I was looking forward to saying goodbye.

"Jeez, Parker, you look like someone stole your lunch money and gave you a wedgie," Mickey said as I walked into the rehab facility on Friday morning.

Apparently, I wasn't very good at hiding my emotions.

"Well, it *is* Burt's last day with us," I said, deflecting the humor onto Burt while avoiding any attempt at a serious conversation. "How do you expect me to feel?"

As I pedaled the stationary bike, I lost myself in thoughts of the case. When the session was over, the four of us went out for coffee.

"Well, Burt," said Joe, "we're going to miss having you there."

"Yeah," Mickey said. "Now we won't have a fourth person for pinochle."

After finishing my decaf coffee, I took Burt aside and gave him the heart-shaped squeeze ball. "Thanks again for your help with the case. You made a great detective."

"I was glad to help. Maybe we could take in a classic car show sometime?"

"I'd like that."

* * *

When I got back to my hotel room, I took a shower while I tried to think about where the investigation would go from here.

I was at a loss for what to do. Every lead I'd gathered had fizzled out like a firework kept in a flooded storeroom.

I stood in the shower for a long time, letting the water rinse over my body as if it might wash away the disappointment I felt.

As I was getting dressed, I got a text message from Tillie. It said she had some information for me about the mysterious warehouse on Airport Road in Concord.

After the week I'd had so far, the last thing I wanted to do was sit around in my hotel room stewing, so I texted back to say I'd love to meet with her in person to discuss her news if she was available.

Tillie said she was working on location at the Museum of Fine Arts in Boston that day but could meet with me during her lunch break. We arranged to meet in the museum's cafe for lunch.

The traffic was fairly light on Route 93 down to Storrow Drive and the Fenway, and I was parked at the Museum of Fine Arts in under an hour. Since I had given myself a full ninety minutes to get there, I decided to take advantage of the remaining half-hour before my appointment with Tillie by browsing the museum's collections.

Located on Huntington Avenue, the MFA Boston contains more than eight thousand paintings and nearly half a million works of art altogether, making it one of the most comprehensive collections in the world.

After paying my admission fee, I headed through the rotunda toward the Art of Europe wing, pausing to look at Giuseppe Piamontini's impressive bronze reliefs, *The Massacre of the Innocents* and *The Fall of the Giants*. I marveled at how the scenes of violence and destruction this Flemish sculptor depicted seemed to spill out from beyond their marble frames.

Relief sculptures like these works and Donatello's *Madonna of the Clouds* always captivated me. Maybe it's because the technique used to create them is a little bit like detective work. You methodically chip away at a problem, eliminating all the suspects and scenarios that don't work until finally a clear picture of the case emerges.

After looking at these relief sculptures, I climbed the steps to the second floor to check out the museum's main attractions: the paintings from European masters such as Van Gogh, Gauguin, Renoir, and Monet.

When I was an undergraduate at UMass Boston, I would often ride the "T" across the city to take advantage of the museum's free admission for students. Gallery 252, featuring one of the largest collections of Monet's work outside France, was typically the busiest gallery in the building. Yet, when it comes to impressionist art, I was always more partial to Pissarro and his works like *Spring Pasture* and *Pontoise, the Road to Gisors in Winter*, hanging in an adjacent gallery.

To me, the highlight of the museum is Gauguin's twelve-foot-long masterpiece, *Where Do We Come From? What Are We? Where Are We Going?* I spent a few minutes trying to decode the painting's mysteries, with its Tahitian natives depicted in varying proportions and stages of life. I also took in Renoir's famous *Dance at Bougival* before heading back downstairs.

There were two special collections displayed on the museum's first floor. One was a set of works exemplifying the Bauhaus movement, featuring artists such as Paul Klee. The other explored civil rights perspectives from modern English and American artists.

Because I had only a few minutes left until my meeting with Tillie, I skipped the Bauhaus collection and opted for the one on civil rights instead. I was especially moved by the painting *Onward Christian Soldiers* by the British artist Mowbray Odonkor.

Created in 1987 and on loan from the Arts Council Collection in London, it was a self-portrait of the artist in front of a field of red, gold, and green stripes, connoting her parents' homeland of Ghana. The upper-left corner displays the British flag, and below that is a scene of African slaves yoked together and being marched off to a foreign land, with the words "onward Christian soldiers" painted ironically above them. Odonkor's arms are outstretched as if she's on an invisible cross, perhaps suggesting that she feels martyred when considering her identity as a Black woman in Britain.

Another piece that affected me deeply was Norman Rockwell's *Murder in Mississippi*, on loan from the Rockwell Museum in western Massachusetts. This stark painting portrays the murders of civil rights workers Michael Schwerner, James Chaney, and Andrew Goodman in 1964. The painting looks like a black-and-white photo, with the red smear of blood on Chaney's hand and shoulder as he leans on Schwerner for support giving the work its only splash of color. The trio's killers are merely suggested by their shadows on the right-hand side of the canvas.

I didn't realize Rockwell had taken on such an explosive topic. I'd always just associated his art with nostalgia for small-town, apple-pie America.

After musing over these powerful works, it was time for my meeting with Tillie, so I made my way back toward the New American Café near the museum's entrance.

* * *

Tillie had texted to let me know she was sitting near the back of the cafe, wearing a yellow blouse and a tartan-patterned scarf. I found her easily enough among the crowd. We introduced ourselves, and I joined her at her table.

"You're working for the museum now?" I asked.

"Yes. They noticed an anomaly in their financial records, and they asked me to investigate. That's all I can really tell you."

A waitress came by to take our orders. Tillie had the butternut squash soup and the skillet-seared salmon. I had a simple green salad and the pan-roasted chicken breast. We both stuck with water to drink.

"To investigations," I said, toasting her with my water glass.

"To *solving* them," she amended, clinking my glass with hers.

Sure. If you're actually competent at your job.

"So, what did you find out about Minerva Enterprises?" I asked her.

"It was established in Delaware eight years ago as an anonymous limited liability company. Basically, the owner used a law firm specializing in anonymous LLCs to create the business. The law firm is listed as the registered agent for the company, and all company correspondence goes through this firm. Meanwhile, the business owner's information is kept completely private."

"How is that different from a shell company?"

"An anonymous LLC is one way to create a shell company, and many—though not all—are simply fronts or holding companies for certain assets. With privacy at a premium in the Internet Age, Delaware and a few other U.S. states allow people to create anonymous LLCs as a way to protect their identity. There are legitimate reasons why someone might create one. For instance, celebrities, people who have been stalked or abused, or those whose business is sensitive in nature might not want their information to be publicly available. However, this anonymity also provides a good cover for illegal activity, such as money laundering or sheltering assets to avoid tax payments.

"That's why Congress passed the Corporate Transparency Act in 2020. The CTA requires the owners of certain businesses with fewer than twenty employees to provide their name, address, date of birth, and legal ID to the Treasury Department's Financial Crimes Enforcement Network. This information is kept in a private database that's available only to law enforcement agencies, so even the owners of anonymous LLCs can't hide their identity from the police any longer."

"That's interesting. Speaking of owners, were you able to learn who owns Minerva Enterprises or anything else about the business?"

"I wasn't able to learn anything about the nature of the business itself, which leads me to believe it's just a shell company like you suspected. As for the owner, it's possible to identify this information if the company has done business in another state or jurisdiction that doesn't offer the same protections as the state where the business was created. For instance, if you know where to look, you can sometimes find an anonymous LLC mentioned in a public document from another state where the company is legally obligated to disclose information about its beneficial owners."

She continued: "In the case of Minerva Enterprises, I managed to find a bank document from a financial transaction involving the company in New York that identified its owner. His name is..."

She checked her notes.

"...Kyle Hammond."

* * *

After Tillie excused herself so she could return to work, I remained at our table in the cafe for several more minutes, thinking about what she had told me and what it meant.

Hammond owned the warehouse. Yet, he'd set up an anonymous LLC to hide his association with the property.

What secret business was he conducting there behind the scenes?

Maybe the name of his anonymous shell company offered a clue. Minerva was the Roman goddess of wisdom, obviously.

Was there any other special significance to this moniker?

Googling "Minerva" on my phone, I learned that it was also the name of a university in San Francisco; a biotech firm in Waltham, Massachusetts; and several pizza places across New England.

Not exactly the kind of dough that Hammond was likely to be interested in.

The most well-known myth about Minerva concerned her interaction with Arachne, the woman who was brazen enough to declare she was a better weaver than Minerva. The goddess ultimately transformed Arachne into a spider as punishment for her pride, consigned to spend the rest of eternity weaving silk webs.

Was it possible that Hammond's illicit activity involved weaving or textiles in any way?

I wasn't going to solve the mystery sitting in the cafe. But I wasn't ready to return to Manchester, either. I decided to take advantage of being in Boston by paying a visit to my alma mater.

I had no idea if this little side trip would serve as the cure for my desolation. But at least it kept me from being alone in an empty hotel room with thoughts of my failure from the last few days.

*　*　*

The Boston campus of the University of Massachusetts system sits on the Columbia Point peninsula, which juts out into Boston Harbor from the city's Dorchester neighborhood. It feels far removed from the bustle of the main city, almost like a forgotten stepchild.

In fact, although there's a section of the city called South Boston, or "Southie" as it's known to the locals, Dorchester is actually *south* of Southie, even more distant from downtown Boston.

It's a picturesque setting, with views of Boston Harbor from some of the university's buildings. But the campus's remote location, situated nearly a mile from the closest subway stop, and the institutional look and feel of its blocky, red brick buildings serve as a constant reminder that a large contingent of the city's residents wanted nothing to do with it when UMass Boston was created in the 1960s.

The mayor at the time, John F. Collins, argued against building the campus in downtown Boston because a disproportionate amount of valuable real estate was already owned by other colleges and nonprofits that were exempt from paying property taxes. Many of the city's elite private universities, including Boston College, Boston University, and Northeastern, opposed the creation of UMass Boston altogether, viewing it as competition for students.

Ultimately, the UMass Board of Trustees voted twelve to four to accept a proposal by the Boston Redevelopment Authority to build the campus on the site of the city's former landfill. (How's *that* for symbolism?)

As you turn off Morrissey Boulevard and approach the campus, the class divide becomes strikingly apparent.

On the left, you pass by Boston College High School, an exclusive private school for boys, with its sprawling campus and gleaming athletic facilities teeming with activity on weekday afternoons. If you didn't know better, you might mistake Murphy Family Stadium, BC High's impressive, eighteen-hundred-seat football stadium, for the UMass Boston stadium—until you realize UMass Boston no longer *has* a football team.

On the right, you can see the yachts moored across Savin Hill Cove, the sun glistening on the water if the weather is cooperative. Straight ahead is the public university campus with its clunky, prison-like appearance, and the contrast is pretty clear.

The university had made several capital improvements since I attended in the late nineties, including a modern, seventy-five million-dollar Campus Center with stunning views of the harbor that opened in 2004. Further improvements are in the works as well, and they're slowly transforming the appearance of the school's urban campus.

But these improvements didn't exist when I enrolled out of high school.

To be honest, I didn't mind the university's appearance when I was in college. For one thing, I was there to learn, and the education I got was first-rate. What's more, I kind of liked the campus's "underdog" sensibility. I wore it as a badge of honor, as it meshed well with my own upbringing.

Growing up in a blue-collar, middle-class family in rural Massachusetts, I counted myself luckier than many. But when it came time for choosing a college, it quickly became clear that a private institution wasn't an option. We weren't poor enough to qualify for much financial aid, and we weren't rich enough to afford a private college tuition. I wasn't nearly athletic enough to earn a scholarship, and I didn't want to be saddled with a lot of student loan debt upon graduation.

I chose UMass Boston because I wanted to be in the city, surrounded by culture and excitement. Although my options were limited by my family's circumstances, it turned out to be a great match in the end. Not only was I inspired by dynamic and highly accomplished faculty, but the campus culture reinforced the values I'd been raised with: You work hard, you *earn* your accomplishments, and you help those who are less fortunate along the way.

I parked in front of the main administrative building and took a stroll around the campus on foot. I hadn't been back in several years, but as soon as I got out of the car, a rush of memories came back to me.

As I walked past McCormack Hall, I remembered the countless hours I'd spent there putting together *The Mass Media*, the university's well-regarded student newspaper. When the new Campus Center opened, the newspaper's offices moved to that building's third floor. But McCormack had been my home away from home for three years. It's where I first honed my investigative skills, looking to apply some sense of fairness to an often unjust world.

On the basis of this work, I was offered a job at the *Concord Herald* when I graduated. I moved to New Hampshire and began a successful career fighting for the little guy.

As I found myself on the Campus Center lawn, I stopped to take in the view of the surrounding harbor. Because it was mid-June, there weren't many people on campus. I sat in a plastic chair on the lawn facing the harbor, gazing out across the water toward Thompson Island.

I'm a good investigator, I reminded myself.

If I'd lost sight of this notion after the events of the last few days, returning to where I'd first learned my craft had helped affirm it.

When I was in college, I had written an exposé for the student newspaper, uncovering questionable business practices by the vendor who handled food service for the university. The piece had taken me three months to research, and it earned me a coveted Hearst award for student journalism. As a result of that article, campus officials switched vendors the following year.

My inquiries into Hammond's business had hit a stumbling block. But I'd learned over the years that the mark of a good investigator was the ability to adapt and be fluid. When you run into an obstacle in one area, there's likely another path forward somewhere else that can lead to success.

My academic mentor at UMass, Harlan Rhodes, was fond of saying that reporters had to be willing to set aside their egos in the relentless pursuit of truth. You have to keep an open mind, admit what you don't know, and always be willing to learn.

I had been relying on help from others throughout the course of my investigation. But to discover the secrets behind Hammond's business, I needed to draw on even further skill sets that I didn't possess for myself.

After two failed attempts at trying to see what was being transported in the back of the box truck, I realized it was time to bring in another heavy hitter off the bench who could help.

Amalia.

Chapter 18

"We'll need recon," Amalia said when I told her my plan.

"You mean reconnaissance?"

"Yes. We should know what we're likely to encounter beforehand."

Trying to sneak a video camera into the back of the box truck hadn't worked, and I didn't think there was any way I would be able to break into the truck again while it was en route. I figured the only option left for scoping out this aspect of Tree Kings' operation was to follow the truck to its final destination, which I assumed was the company's Pittsburg location, and watch as it was being unloaded.

This would be challenging for many reasons. I would somehow have to infiltrate the company's remote northern compound, breaching who knew how many defenses, and spy on this activity without being seen.

It was the kind of task that called for someone with the skills of Jason Bourne, not Jimmy Breslin.

Fortunately, I had Amalia to help me.

At five feet four, she was hardly a physically imposing figure. Though well-toned, her body was slight, and it was easy for people to underestimate her. But that would be a dangerous mistake.

The only outward sign suggesting that she had survived elite military training and emerged victorious was a small tattoo on her left shoulder of a skull wearing a tan beret—the Army Ranger symbol.

I had never seen her in action before. But Kris had told me about the time when she and Mal had been on vacation in the Caribbean once. They were approached by two large men, well over six feet in height, with more on their minds than polite conversation. The encounter landed both men in a local infirmary—one with cracked ribs and a broken nose and the other with a crushed windpipe.

With Amalia serving as my backup, I felt a lot better about my chances.

We were sitting at a table in the Tipsy Moose after hours on Monday evening. Mal was closing the place, so she let me hang around while she wiped down the bar and restocked for the next day's lunch shift. Then, we retreated to one corner to discuss our plan.

"If we can get an advance look at the Pittsburg facility before we follow the truck there," she said, "we'll be in a much better position to succeed."

"I know a way we can do that."

"How?"

"We pretend to be commercial real estate appraisers."

During the course of my investigative work, there were many times when I needed a false pretense to take pictures, occasionally on someone's private property. I'd found that posing as an appraiser supplied the perfect cover.

Real estate appraisers provide an objective, unbiased estimate of a property's value. They do this by gathering information about the property itself—such as its size, location, condition, and amenities—and then comparing this information to similar properties in the area. Appraisers play a critical role in tax assessments, lease negotiations, and mortgage lending decisions, among other scenarios.

In preparing their reports, appraisers have to find and evaluate nearby "comps," or properties that are analogous in nature to the ones they're reporting on. To assess a commercial property they think would make a good comp, it's not uncommon for appraisers to show up at the property and ask the occupants if they can have a look around, maybe take some photos for their report.

I'd even had phony business cards printed for this purpose. The cards read:

CHARLES "GUS" DUPIN
Appraiser
"Bringing value to your real estate transactions"

"We can say we'd like to take a quick look at the facility for an appraisal we're doing on a similar commercial property in the area," I explained. "That would give us a valid reason to take photos and even see inside the building. We can tell them you're apprenticing with me, and nobody should question it."

"That sounds great," Amalia replied. "Next, we'll need to define our PIRs."

"Our what?"

"Sorry—Primary Intelligence Requirements. These are the main objectives for our reconnaissance mission. What information will help us achieve our goals most effectively?"

"You mean like the placement of security cameras, that sort

of thing?"

"Yes, exactly," Amalia said, taking out a pen and a server's notepad. "We'll also want to know how many employees are working on the property and where they're likely to be. We'll want to know who's armed and with what weapons, if possible. And we'll want to identify all the ways to get in and out of the facility, where they lead, whether they're locked and how."

As Mal was talking, she wrote down each objective.

"You said the truck makes its weekly deliveries on Thursday?" she asked.

"Yeah, that's right."

"Ideally, we'd want to do our recon on a Thursday as well, so we could see how many people will be there on the day of the week for our actual mission."

"That makes sense. But I don't want to wait that long. That would add another whole week to the process. I already wasted time last week on a plan that didn't work."

"All right, we'll go on my day off from the bar tomorrow. But you should know that staffing at the facility could be completely different when we do this for real on Thursday."

* * *

I picked up Amalia at nine-thirty the next morning. Although we weren't doing our reconnaissance on the correct day of the week, we wanted at least to observe the facility around the same time of day as I assumed the box truck would arrive on Thursday.

Instead of her usual jeans and crop-top tee shirt, Mal was wearing a professional-looking blouse and a pair of black chinos.

"Thanks for doing this," I said. "It's not too early to be leaving after you closed the bar last night, is it?"

"Oh please. In Ranger School I functioned on just two hours of sleep a day. Six hours is a luxury."

It was nearly a four-hour drive from Manchester to the Tree Kings' remote outpost in Pittsburg, which makes up the entire northern tip of New Hampshire.

The largest town by area in all of New England, Pittsburg is nearly three hundred square miles in size, yet it has only eight hundred residents—making it among the most sparsely populated towns in the state. Pittsburg shares a border with Maine along its eastern edge and with Quebec to the north and west.

Driving to the northernmost reaches of the state made me realize just what a big country this is.

Once you travel north of the White Mountains, there isn't much in the way of civilization. When you get beyond the throngs of vacationers in the Lakes Region and the streams of hikers in the mountains, there are long stretches with nothing to see but trees—and New Hampshire isn't even a very large state. You could fit about nine New Hampshires into the state of Idaho alone, and you could fit almost two Idahos into California.

To pass the time, I asked Amalia about her Army experience, which we hadn't talked about much before.

"What was it like going through Ranger School?"

"The training is designed to test your limits physically and mentally. You're always either hungry or tired. As long as you're one or the other, you're okay. It's when you're *both* that people really struggle."

"What did the training consist of?"

"There were three phases, each lasting for twenty days. During the first phase, we had to complete squad-level missions in groups of eight to ten people, and everyone had a chance to be the squad leader. In phase two, we moved into the mountains, so there was the added challenge of functioning in uneven terrain at higher altitudes. We also had to complete missions with four squads working together as a platoon of thirty to forty people. Phase three was a water stage, where we were operating in swamps. In phase three we functioned as a company, which is three platoons working together—so, a hundred people or more.

"Our missions consisted of recon, raids, and assaults. We were given objectives and a topographical map before each mission, and we had to plan and execute the operation. That included stealth movement to each target, completing the mission, and then moving on to a new patrol base. We would only be given one or two meals a day, and we were operating on just a few hours of sleep. Often we would be covering ten to twelve miles of ground in a day."

"Was it tough for you as a woman?"

"You have no idea."

"Want to tell me about it? Or, would you rather not?"

"No, it's okay. Carrying more than sixty pounds of equipment during each mission was a challenge, but even harder than that was dealing with the egos of the men who were either scared of being shown up by a girl or convinced I was a liability, no matter what I did to prove myself. To succeed in our missions, we had to trust each other. I had to go above and beyond what the others did to earn that trust, and so I would volunteer for extra tasks just to make myself invaluable to the team."

"What would you say is the biggest takeaway from your experience?"

"Just the euphoria I felt when I finished stage three, and the confidence I gained as a result. After going through that whole experience, I felt like I was ready to face anything."

*　*　*

The Tree Kings' Pittsburg facility was located on a side road off Route 3 just north of the First Connecticut Lake. The road dead-ended in front of the facility, which was built in the midst of a forest clearing. The facility consisted of a one-story main building to the left and a massive, two-story garage on the right. The main building and garage were connected within a single structure.

"So, how do you want to play this?" Amalia asked.

"Let's start taking photos of the exterior like we belong here. If someone comes out and questions what we're doing, I'll do the talking."

We got out of the car and headed in opposite directions. Amalia circled the building to the right, around the garage, while I went around to the left.

A tall, well-proportioned guy in a plain gray tee shirt, jeans, and hiking boots emerged from the front door and walked toward me with quick strides. He was about six-foot-two with spiky dark hair, a weathered face, and a callous look.

"Who are you, and what do you think you're doing?" he asked me.

I produced a phony business card and offered it to him. "Gus Dupin, how are you? I'm a real estate appraiser. Do you mind if my colleague and I take a few photos of your property for a report we're putting together for a client?"

"Yeah, I mind. This is private property."

"Yes, but you're also a contractor for the state, which makes you a public entity in the eyes of the law," I bluffed. "Don't worry, we'll be out of your hair in no time. You won't even know we're here."

"I don't *want* you here. Did you not understand me? Now beat it."

"Are you the property owner?"

"No."

"Well, don't you want your boss to get fair market value when he eventually sells this property or leaves it to his family? Appraisals like this are how that happens. We're not interrupting anything, right? And you're not doing anything illegal or improper?"

"Of course not."

"Then what's your concern?"

He still seemed unsure.

"Listen, help me out here, man—one professional to another," I said, leaning in closer. "There aren't a lot of similar commercial properties in this town that I can use as comps in an appraisal. It would really mean a lot to me if we could use this property in our report."

I took out my wallet, produced a twenty-dollar bill, and held it out to him.

"For your troubles. We'd just like a few photos of the exterior, and a quick look inside the building and the garage—and then we're done. What do you say?"

He plucked the money from my fingers and gestured for us to follow him inside.

* * *

On the drive back to Manchester, Amalia and I compared notes about what we'd seen.

"I didn't notice any other employees at the facility today except for Mr. Tee," I said.

"Mr. T?"

"Sorry, Mr. Tee Shirt Guy."

"Yes, but that doesn't mean we won't see anyone else when we come back on Thursday. We have to be ready for anything. Did you see the bulge in the waistband of his jeans? I'm pretty sure he was carrying a gun."

"Wow, I'm glad you were there with me today. That's something I never would have noticed myself."

Unlike the main Tree Kings facility in Concord, which looked like a showcase for the company's business, its northern outpost was all about utility.

The inside of the main building consisted of a few office spaces in the front and a storage area toward the rear. It was linked to the two-story garage and warehousing space by a connecting steel door. This garage area, which was about fifty feet deep and thirty feet wide, had a second-story catwalk running along its back wall, accessed by a set of stairs on the left.

The catwalk afforded a view of the open garage space, and it ended at what looked like a raised office or additional storage space in the right rear corner of the structure. Unfortunately, there were no windows in the garage.

Around the back of the building, an iron staircase led to a steel door which I assumed opened into the raised office space above the garage. An array of heavy forestry equipment was parked behind the facility. I noticed a feller buncher, two harvesters, a log loader, a stump splitter, a mulcher, and several all-terrain vehicles.

"If we're lucky," I said, "they'll unload the truck in the dirt driveway in front of the building. If that's the case, I should be able to watch from the woods easily enough. More likely, though, they'll drive the truck into the garage to unload it, in which case I'll have to figure out how to sneak into the garage without being spotted in order to see what's happening."

"Accessing the garage from the main building doesn't seem practical," Amalia said. "The chances are pretty high they'll see you come through the door."

"That leaves the stairs up to the rear entrance and the elevated catwalk," I said. "If the door at the top of the stairs is locked, I should be able to pick it without a problem. I just hope it's not deadbolted from the inside."

"Approaching the staircase, you'll be exposed," Mal observed. "I noticed outdoor cameras in both the front and rear of the facility. Your best course of action is to approach the stairs from the side of the building. But if someone is monitoring the cameras, you'll be visible as you climb. I'll hang back and provide cover from the woods."

* * *

I dropped off Amalia at our apartment building and headed for the hotel. When I got back to my room, I just wanted to crash after driving for so many hours. But first, I was determined to check my email and catch up on the news of the day.

I sat on the bed with my laptop. Before logging in, I turned on the TV and flipped through the channels, looking for something that could serve as comforting background noise. After the near encounters I'd had with death in the last few weeks, I'd found complete silence to be unsettling, especially at night.

The Sox didn't play for another half hour yet. But on WSBK-TV out of Boston—the old Channel 38 when I was growing up—I found an old episode of *The Three Stooges*. It was the one where the Stooges sneak into a country club to practice golfing: "Three Little Beers." To gain access, they pretend to be reporters by using knobs torn from bathroom fixtures as press badges. In one of the trio's best-ever gags, Moe's and Larry's knobs are marked "press," but Curly's reads "pull."

I tried that bit once when I was a beat reporter by showing my press badge and saying (in Curly's voice): "Pull." It didn't go over well.

There was nothing of interest in my email. However, as I was browsing the news, a brief item from the *Herald's* website caught my attention. It said the Missing Persons division of the Concord Police Department was looking for a local man named John Rizzo who hadn't been seen since the previous Friday, and his family was worried.

I immediately thought of Hammond and his goons.

Rizzo approaches Hammond and offers him information in exchange for money. He tells Hammond about the camera he's been asked to plant in the back of the box truck. Then later that week, he disappears without a trace.

The timing seemed too much of a coincidence not to be related. I doubted the police would find Rizzo alive.

In Rizzo's last remarks to me, he'd implied that I was foolish for trusting a known criminal in a business matter.

Should've heeded his own advice, I thought wryly.

Chapter 19

As Yogi Berra once said, it was like déjà vu all over again.

I was sitting in my rented Ford Fusion on Thursday morning, following the box truck from Tree Kings at a safe distance as it made the weekly pilgrimage up Route 93 toward what I assumed was the company's Pittsburg facility.

This time, however, there was a key difference. Amalia was following several car lengths behind me in her jeep convertible. An M4 carbine rifle sat on the seat beside her, and a Beretta nine-millimeter pistol was holstered on her waist.

We had been waiting for the truck to leave since five-thirty that morning. Although it hadn't departed until after eight o'clock the other times I was watching, we weren't taking any chances. After the previous week's surveillance debacle, anything was possible—and we wanted to be prepared for whatever contingencies might arise.

As it did the first time I was watching, the truck stopped at the nondescript warehouse near the Concord airport first, where it disappeared inside for nearly half an hour before resuming its journey. It made another stop at the Growth Potential facility, then continued north—this time without pausing at the diner in Campton or anywhere else.

Apparently, the driver wasn't about to let the truck out of his sight again.

Because I thought I knew the truck's ultimate destination, I could afford to hang back at quite a distance. That served us well as we turned onto Route 3 just north of Franconia Notch and traffic became more sparse.

It was after one p.m. when the box truck finally turned off Route 3 after the First Connecticut Lake and headed down the side road toward the Tree Kings' northernmost facility.

I stayed back pretty far, pulling my car into a hollow area off the side of the road and hiking the final quarter-mile stretch toward the building on foot. I didn't see Mal behind me, but I knew she must have been lurking there somewhere.

As I approached the compound, I used the trees on the side of the road for cover. There was no sign of the truck outside the facility, so I assumed it had driven into the large, two-story garage to the right of the main building.

Remaining in the shadow of the trees, I edged along the perimeter of the compound until I was opposite the side of the garage.

I looked around carefully, but there was no sign of anyone outside the facility. Acutely aware of how exposed I was, I sprinted from the edge of the woods to the side wall of the garage, then edged along the wall and around the corner to the base of the iron staircase. I crept noiselessly up the stairs to the door. I tried the handle, but not surprisingly, it was locked.

Within a few seconds, I had picked the lock. I opened the door a crack and let my eyes adjust to the dimness inside.

I was looking into a dingy storage room, filled with boxes of spare parts for the forestry equipment used by Tree Kings personnel and serviced in the garage space below.

I slipped into the storage room and closed the exterior door behind me. An interior door across the room stood ajar, leading to the catwalk overlooking the garage as I had assumed. I tiptoed out onto the catwalk and surveyed the scene beneath me.

The box truck was parked with its back toward me, the rear of the truck facing open. Inside, I could see that some of its floorboards were missing. Two men—the driver of the truck and a second man wearing a bright orange vest—were carrying objects from the back of the truck and transferring them to an oversized duffle bag strapped to the back of an ATV.

From where I was crouched, I couldn't see clearly what they were carrying.

I took a small pair of binoculars from my pocket and held them up to my eyes.

In an instant, I could see everything—and I realized with a gasp what the secret cargo was that I had been wondering about for the last few weeks.

Guns.

They were transporting weapons in the truck's hidden compartment.

I knew next to nothing about various types of firearms. But from what I could tell, it looked like an assortment of handguns and automatic rifles. There were several dozen pieces altogether.

I carefully inserted my phone into a cradle attached to the binoculars so I could record a sharp, magnified video of the criminals' activity.

As focused as I was on the activity below, I didn't notice that someone was standing behind me until I felt the muzzle of a gun pressed into my back.

A flat voice from behind me said: "Move and you're dead."

* * *

I slowly raised my hands above my head, and the thug standing behind me snatched my phone and binoculars.

"Real estate appraiser, huh? I should have known better."

It was Mr. Tee Shirt Guy from the other day. This time, he was wearing a black tee shirt—and he looked even less friendly than before.

He called out to the others with a sneer: "Hey guys, look what I found!"

The two men who were unloading the guns from the truck turned around, and the truck's driver grinned malevolently when he recognized me.

I was marched outside at gunpoint and led to the heavy logging machinery parked around the back of the compound.

"Okay," the gunman said, "it's time to find out what you know. Shall we use the stump splitter or the mulcher?"

"Wait a minute," said the guy in the orange vest. "You're not actually gonna…"

"Hey Dustin," the gunman said, "maybe you should go back inside and wait if you're squeamish."

Dustin didn't respond. But he didn't move, either.

"I'm going to ask you some questions now," the gunman said. "And I want the truth."

"What difference does it make?" I said. "You're just going to kill me anyway."

"Yeah, but it's up to *you* how unpleasant the experience will be. Tell me what I'm looking for, and I'll make it much faster and less painful. Otherwise…"

He gestured to the driver of the box truck, who climbed into the cab of the mulcher and turned on the ignition.

As the mulcher blades whirred to life, just their high-pitched whine itself seemed to cut into me. The thought of what the actual blades would do sent spasms throughout my body.

"Are you alone?" the gunman asked.

"Yes, I came here alone," I said quietly. Technically, that was correct. Amalia had followed me in her own vehicle.

Where was Mal? I thought. *My god, I hope she's coming.* I felt a sharp stab of panic in my chest as I suddenly worried that she'd been ambushed herself and was unable to come to my aid.

"So, what are you doing with all those guns?" I asked. I was trying to stall, of course—but I was also genuinely curious. I didn't want to die without at least understanding more of the puzzle.

"*I'll* ask the questions," the gunman said. "What were you doing spying on us? Who do you work for?"

The noise of the mulcher was so loud, I didn't even hear the crack of the rifle. I only realized that Amalia had fired—and her bullet had found its mark—when I saw the gunman's head explode in a spray of red.

The driver of the box truck saw the same thing I did, and he was quick to react. So quick, in fact, that Mal's second bullet missed him completely as he dropped to the floor of the mulcher cab and pulled out his own gun, returning her fire.

I had no idea what his background was. But my money was on Amalia in that exchange.

Sensing an opportunity in the confusion, the guy in the orange vest, Dustin, hopped onto a nearby ATV and sped off toward a forest trail head behind the compound.

I ran to one of the other ATVs and was surprised to find the key was in the ignition. I'd never actually driven one before, but aside from a throttle, a wider wheel base, and a great deal more speed, I imagined it wasn't much different from mountain biking—and I had plenty of experience doing that.

As I took off in pursuit of Dustin, from the corner of my eye I saw the box truck driver spin from a bullet strike to the torso and slump against the door to the mulcher cab. The stunned look on his face was the last thing I noticed before I found myself enveloped by thick trees in the woods.

* * *

The guy on the ATV ahead of me had a few advantages. He was familiar with the vehicle and how it operated. He also knew these logging trails well.

My only advantage—and it was a big one—was that I was pissed.

I'd just had my third brush with death in as many weeks. That made me fearless with anger.

I crouched low in an aerodynamic position and made my legs into springs by keeping my weight on the balls of my feet, absorbing the shock of the bumps with my knees. I leaned into the corners and accelerated out of them, willing the machine beneath me to go faster.

Under different circumstances, I might have enjoyed the rush of speeding over the rough terrain. But I was hyper focused on pursuing the rogue forester in front of me, chewing up the precious yards that separated us like Pac Man gobbling pellets in a maze.

I was only a few yards behind Dustin's ATV when the trail

veered sharply to the right. I wasn't anticipating the turn, which forced me to slow down, and I lost ground again.

This pattern—a few tantalizing yards closer, followed by a few frustrating yards lost back—kept repeating for at least a mile.

Then the crook ahead of me hit a large bump, and it almost dislodged him from his ATV. Though he managed to regain his balance, he'd been slowed enough that I was now right behind him, nearly close enough to touch him.

As he turned into a bend toward the left, I cut the corner aggressively, closing the gap so that the right front tire of my ATV was even with the left rear tire of his machine.

I steered into him, and the back of his ATV kicked out, throwing him off the machine and into the woods.

I didn't know if he was armed, so I hopped off my own vehicle and approached him cautiously.

The orange-vested hoodlum sprang up off the ground and pulled a serrated pruning knife from his belt. He lunged at me with the knife.

In a move that was more reflex than skill, I caught his right forearm in my left hand.

With my own right forearm, I smashed the bridge of his nose, and he crumpled in a heap at my feet.

* * *

A few hours later, Amalia and I were talking with an agent from the federal Bureau of Alcohol, Tobacco, Firearms and Explosives outside the Tree Kings' northern facility.

We had no choice but to call nine-one-one in the aftermath of what happened, and the state police were sent to investigate.

I didn't say anything about my suspicions of the governor or how I thought his administration might have been connected.

We told the staties what we'd witnessed and what happened to us as a result. After examining the guns in the garage, the state trooper in charge called in the ATF.

The agent we were speaking with, Carol Gilmartin, was a tall, no-nonsense woman with a scar across her left cheek. I wondered what she'd done to earn the scar—and what had become of the person who'd given it to her.

"I just got off the phone with Detective Connor from the Concord Police Department," Agent Gilmartin said. "He backs up your story."

Gilmartin had been skeptical of our account, even though Amalia and I had been questioned separately about what happened and our stories had matched. Gilmartin was inclined to think we were working with the crooks whom Mal had shot and that maybe we'd had a falling out, dispatched them, and then invented a story to cover our tracks.

"So we're free to go now?"

"Yes, but don't make yourselves scarce. There's a good chance I'll be back in touch with more questions."

"And you'll let me know what you learn about how the guns tie into Tree Kings' operations?"

"Oh yeah, you'll be the first person I call. In fact, I have you on speed dial now."

I'm not saying I preferred the prospect of facing the tree mulcher. But Agent Gilmartin's sarcasm was pretty cutting itself.

As Amalia and I left the Tree Kings outpost and walked back to where we'd left our vehicles, I tapped her on the shoulder with my fist. "Thanks for saving my life."

"Don't mention it, neighbor. All in a day's work."

Chapter 20

Cardiac rehab was rough the next day, to say the least. Chasing down a fleeing criminal on an ATV had required the use of muscles in my arms and legs that I rarely exerted, and I was sore from the effort.

"You look like an old man this morning," Joe said.

"Yeah, you look like us today," Mickey added.

After finishing up at the hospital, I joined Detective Connor for a late breakfast in downtown Concord. As he slathered his stack of pancakes in maple syrup, I eyed his plate with jealousy. After the last few weeks I'd experienced, it took every bit of willpower I had to limit my order to fresh fruit and a glass of tomato juice.

"That guy whose clock you cleaned yesterday was singing to the feds all evening," Connor said, telling me what he'd learned from ATF Agent Gilmartin earlier that morning. "Turns out Hammond's forest management company has been smuggling guns across the border into Canada for years."

"No kidding?"

"Yeah. Apparently they've been using their forestry work as a way to access the border without arousing suspicion. They figured no one would think twice if a border patrol agent or a drone noticed a state forestry contractor working near the border. They'd have employees leave bags full of guns in remote wooded areas along the border, and their contacts in Canada would retrieve the weapons. Fully automatic firearms are illegal in Canada, so they could fetch thousands of dollars for the weapons on the black market. When a nationwide freeze on handgun sales went into effect throughout Canada in 2022, that opened up an even larger market for illegal firearms."

"So how big was their operation?"

"That guy you captured doesn't know the exact numbers, but he said they were smuggling in excess of a hundred guns a week."

I let out a low whistle. "Hundreds of thousands of dollars in undeclared income every week? No wonder Hammond wanted that state contract so badly. It gave him the perfect cover for his smuggling operation."

"Speaking of Hammond, he's disappeared. Someone must have tipped him off that the feds were onto him. No one has seen him since yesterday afternoon."

"Did the guy who's been talking to the feds know anything about Mark's and Maggie's murders?"

"No, but the ATF has opened an entire investigation into Hammond's businesses. They've subpoenaed everything. We're piggy-backing onto their investigation, and we hope we'll learn something that ties Hammond to the murders of your friend and your client's husband."

"Where did Hammond get the guns?"

"The feds don't know yet. But it looks like he stored them in that warehouse on Airport Road that you were talking about and then transported them north in the secret compartment of the truck you were following. Probably as a precaution in case the truck was ever stopped and searched for some reason."

* * *

The information that Connor had gleaned from Agent Gilmartin answered a lot of the questions I'd been wrestling with for the last few weeks.

I now knew why that state forestry contract had been so important to Hammond—and why he was willing to kill to protect his secret. Most importantly, the ATF's investigation would hopefully help the Concord police close the book on the murders of Maggie and Mark.

But there was still a key thread that needed resolving. So far, there was no evidence connecting Gordon or members of his administration with Hammond's illegal activity.

I had no doubt that Gordon was somehow directly involved. Maybe he was even the ringleader of the whole operation.

Rigging the bidding process to make sure Hammond's company continued to win the contract for managing the state forest lands abutting the Canadian border didn't just start and end with Lemay, the procurement director. Hammond was far too dialed into everything that had been going on: that Mark was working with Maggie, that the feds had just gotten involved the day before. This was all inside information that could only come from someone higher up in Gordon's administration.

Plus, Hammond and Gordon had a clear connection dating back to when they were fraternity brothers at Dartmouth. Although this fact wasn't conclusive, it was at least strongly suggestive that they were working together.

But proving it was another matter. I was no closer to doing

so now than I was when I first suspected Mark and Maggie had been murdered.

To make things worse, I was out of new ideas. I had no clue how to uncover Gordon's involvement.

Maybe it was all the thinking I'd been doing about forestry lately. But it was the only plan I could come up with at the moment.

Time to shake some trees and see what falls out.

* * *

Before heading back to my hotel in Manchester, I stopped by the *Herald* offices and talked with Bellows.

"Hiya, boss. Have I got a scoop for you."

I told him the broad strokes. To report the story, he pulled an enterprising young reporter named Samantha Gunderson off the feature she was writing for Sunday's edition about a seventy-three-year-old grandmother who'd hiked all forty-eight of the state's four-thousand-foot peaks earlier that year.

Bellows, Sam, and I retreated to a conference room in the *Herald* offices, where I described in vivid detail the events of the previous day and how I believed they were connected to Gordon's administration.

"Let me see if I understand you correctly," Bellows said when I finished. "You think the governor of our state is somehow involved in this scheme to smuggle guns across the border into Canada? But you don't have any proof?"

"No, I don't have any proof. But I think the facts of the story are quite compelling in themselves. I think the citizens of New Hampshire might appreciate knowing, for instance, that Hammond's company only held the state contract because of a bidding process that both the losing bidder *and* the governor's deputy chief of staff believed to be fraudulent. Yet, when these concerns were raised, they were quickly brushed under the rug. Readers might also find it interesting that Hammond and Gordon were not just friends but fraternity brothers in college. And finally, if you do some investigating, I think you'll find this was the story that Maggie was working on when she and her main source, Deputy Chief of Staff Mark Bowman, were tragically killed in an accident the police are now calling second-degree murder."

Bellows sat quietly for a long time, making a tent with his fingers while he thought.

"Sam, I'm going to get you access to Maggie's files, so you can try to confirm Parker's suspicions," he said finally. "I agree with Parker there's a big story here, but we have to be very careful in how we report it. Let's stay away from mentioning the fraternity connection unless we can establish a stronger and more recent relationship between the two men. Perhaps you'll turn up something in the course of your own research that Parker couldn't, simply by virtue of your access as a member of the press. Or maybe someone who knows more will see this story and be willing to talk."

* * *

Flush with success from my meeting with Bellows, I drove back to my hotel room and put into motion phase two of my rudimentary plan.

I opened my laptop and searched for the website of every state government agency I could think of, beginning with the Department of Administrative Services. I looked for the email addresses of every employee I could find. I sent them all a carefully worded message that I hoped would prompt someone to become a confidential source, revealing new information that could jump-start my investigation:

"If you have any knowledge of Governor Gordon meeting, interacting with, or having a personal relationship with Kyle Hammond or any other employees of the state contractor Tree Kings, please let me know."

The words "personal relationship" made me think of Callie, and I wondered how she was doing. I called to check in with her, but I got her voice mail, and so I left a message:

"Hi Callie, it's Parker calling. I've been thinking about you a lot, and I hope you're doing okay. If you'd like to get together again, or even if you're just looking for someone to talk to, give me a call."

Then I closed my laptop and lay down on the bed. I intended to clear my head by watching a few minutes of mindless TV, but the strain of the last few weeks caught up to me—and I was soon asleep.

* * *

I woke up a few hours later to the sound of my cell phone ringing. At first I thought it was Callie calling me back, and I almost levitated off the bed.

But when I saw the name on the caller ID, my joy was extinguished like a flame in outer space.

"Parker, this is Bryce Kilcullen calling from Governor Gordon's office. The governor has learned of your little email stunt from earlier today, and he'd like to meet with you. Be in his office Monday morning, ten o'clock sharp."

Chapter 21

As I was checking my email and browsing the news on Monday morning, I noticed that Sam's initial report on the gun smuggling ring was the lead story on the *Herald's* website.

The story didn't go much beyond the details I'd given her. But it explained how the choice of Tree Kings as a state contractor had been mired in controversy. It also highlighted the key role that Amalia and I had played in uncovering the scheme.

Chief of Staff Bryce Kilcullen was quoted as saying the governor was shocked—*shocked*—to learn that Hammond had taken advantage of his position as a state contractor to commit these heinous crimes. He adamantly denied that anyone in Gordon's administration knew of these illegal activities, or that there was any impropriety in awarding the state contract to Tree Kings.

After reading the story, I was sure of two things. The first was that Sam wasn't done investigating and would continue digging to find some clear connection between Hammond and Gordon.

The second thing I was certain about was that Sam's story was going to make my meeting with the governor that morning even more uncomfortable.

***

The Monday morning traffic up to Concord was heavy, but it moved steadily. By a quarter to ten, I was turning onto Park Street and parking beside the State House building, opposite St. Paul's Church.

Built in the early nineteenth century and set back from Concord's main street, the New Hampshire State House is a three-story white granite structure that rises impressively from behind a tree-studded green. The building features a classical Greek-style facade and a cupola topped with a modest gold dome. A black marble statue of Daniel Webster, New Hampshire's favorite son, stands proudly before the front steps.

The mid-morning sun glinted off the State House dome as I approached the building uneasily. My heart felt like I'd just run a five K, and my nerves felt like live wires downed in a thunderstorm.

I had been inside the State House building many times before when I was a reporter for the *Herald*. In fact, I had interviewed Gordon there once, almost twenty years earlier.

It was back when I was still on the political beat, before I became an investigative reporter. Gordon was a rising star in the state Senate at the time, and I had been asked by the city news editor to write a profile of him.

Of course, that was long before I suspected he was involved in a criminal conspiracy that included multiple homicides.

Even during that interview, which was hardly adversarial in nature, Gordon had displayed an air of smug superiority that

I'd found intimidating.

When his face twitched in amusement as he noticed my discount-rack suit, I was reduced in my head to a stuttering teenager.

As he boasted about leading his high school lacrosse team to the New England prep school championship while at Exeter, barely acknowledging me while wrapped in his own self-importance, I was reminded of the time my public high school debate team faced off against Williston Northampton, an elite private academy, and I overheard the opposing team members snickering that we would be mowing their lawns someday.

When the interview was over and Gordon said in a perfunctory tone, "Thank you, Peter, it was a pleasure speaking with you," I thought about all the years I'd spent waiting tables at a local country club to put myself through college—and how I'd been invisible to most of the members.

It didn't matter that I'd graduated with honors near the top of my college class, or that—on a purely intellectual plane—I was probably at least Gordon's equal. The sense of privilege that people like Gordon carried was its own sort of weapon. It chipped away at my sense of self-worth and left me feeling vulnerable, even before factoring in the very real danger that Gordon now posed.

Add in the notion that Gordon himself might be a stone-cold killer—albeit without getting his own hands dirty, as that would be beneath him—and it was no wonder I was apprehensive as I ascended the State House steps.

I wasn't afraid of being attacked outside the building, or disappearing for good once I'd gone inside. There were far too many people milling around for me to feel like I was entering a lion's den.

However, I was also vividly aware of the power dynamic that existed in this seat of state government—and how Gordon could crush me any time he wanted just by picking up the phone.

I had seen his petty vindictiveness firsthand after the interview that took place nearly two decades before.

I had written what I thought was a well-balanced article about Gordon's early life, his education, and his success as a venture capitalist before entering the political arena. I quoted him about the pride he felt in being a "self-made" businessman, but for context I noted that he was able to launch his own business with the help of a two million dollar loan from his father.

Apparently, that truth didn't sit well with him.

Imagine how Gordon would have reacted if I'd kept a sentence in the story that I had written but quickly deleted, in which I pointed out that most people could be "self-made" with resources like that.

Gordon had called the *Herald's* publisher and demanded that I be fired for writing what he called a "hit piece." Luckily, my boss at the time was Bellows, who didn't take kindly to receiving personnel advice from a state lawmaker.

Bellows had interceded and defended me to the publisher, and the whole thing eventually blew over. But that was also when newspapers wielded a bigger influence in our society. The *Herald* was still making money in those days, and the publisher could afford to tell Gordon to go make love to an electrical socket.

I wondered if that would have happened in our current environment. With newspapers forced to scrounge for every quarter like a kid rifling through the coin return slots in an '80s-era arcade, how many publishers would have the gumption to push back against someone in a position of power like that now?

When I was let go from the *Herald*, the newspaper was coming off its second straight year of major losses. The owners sold the paper to a national syndicate, which proceeded to lay off half the employees. Only a barebones staff of local reporters remained. The *Herald* now relied on wire service reports for all of its national news coverage and much of its state news reporting as well.

Though Bellows and his team were doing heroic work with the resources they had, the shortage of reporters likely meant there was a spate of corruption going on within state and local governments that wasn't being revealed. It was a familiar story playing out in communities across the country.

What were the establishments that could protect us from rampant corruption today? Where were the institutions that would help preserve our democracy?

The governor's office was on the second floor of the State House building. I took the south staircase up to the second floor, pausing on the way to look at a giant mural depicting Pickett's Charge during the third day of the Battle of Gettysburg in 1863.

Copied from a larger work by the French artist Paul Philippoteaux, the mural's battle scene fascinated me, and I always managed to discover some small new detail as I studied it. On this morning, my eye was drawn to two men fighting hand to hand in the lower right corner. An older man in a uniform of a color that matched his gray whiskers—a Rebel soldier—lay on the ground, pointing his pistol at the overmatched Union soldier.

Farther to the left of this scene, two Union soldiers stood by their fallen comrade. One of them was removing the wounded man's foot from the stirrups of his horse. *To treat the soldier?* I wondered. *Or use the horse?* The men's faces weren't detailed enough to read their expressions, but I could imagine the fear, the anguish, that lay there.

With a hint of shame, I realized I was stalling to avoid my inevitable confrontation with Gordon. I pulled myself away from the mural and continued up the stairs.

* * *

As I entered the antechamber to the governor's office, Gordon's secretary looked up from a stack of papers on her desk and regarded me through stylish, tortoise-shell glasses.

"I'm Parker Hanson. The governor requested a meeting with me?"

She indicated a door on her right. "In there."

I walked in to find Gordon seated behind a mammoth oak desk the size of a small yacht. Kilcullen was sitting on a leather settee off to the side of the room, cradling a champagne flute with what looked like a mimosa in both hands. Neither of them rose to greet me.

On a small coffee table in front of the settee was a lavish breakfast spread with smoked salmon, sliced strawberries, mini pancakes, crème fraiche, and bowls of what I assumed was red and black caviar.

"Mr. Hanson, have a seat," Gordon said, pointing to the two wingback chairs facing his desk.

I chose the chair on the left and sank into the upholstery. *Mr. Hanson.* I felt like I was in the fourth grade and had been summoned to the principal's office … if the principal had the power to make me disappear with a simple phone call.

Gordon was an imposing man in his mid-fifties, with salt-and-pepper hair swept back from his face. Although not particularly tall at just under six feet, he was still an intimidating presence. His broad, blocky features looked like they were chiseled from hard clay, like a golem.

"Bryce tells me you've been investigating the smuggling of firearms into Canada by one of our state contractors—and that it was you who ultimately uncovered this scheme."

"Yes, that's right."

"Needless to say, we were both stunned to learn of this discovery."

I didn't respond.

"Bryce also says you have some crazy theory that somehow my office was involved. I don't know where you got such a far-fetched idea, but my staff and I have nothing to hide. Let's resolve this nonsense once and for all. Is there anything you'd like to ask me?"

"Sure. Are you guilty?"

Gordon and Kilcullen exchanged glances, and they both chuckled.

To me, it seemed a little forced.

"I suppose you're aware that Kyle Hammond and I were fraternity brothers while we both attended Dartmouth around the same time. It's true that we knew each other then. But we haven't stayed in touch very much, and I haven't seen him in years."

I refrained from speaking, waiting for him to continue.

"From the look on your face, I can see that you don't believe me. What will it take to convince you? Would you like to see phone records?"

"All that would prove is that you're smart enough not to use official channels when communicating. And frankly, that's not a very high bar to clear."

"Parker, why don't you help yourself to some caviar," Kilcullen said, pointing to the spread on the table in front of him.

Apparently, Bryce was playing the role of the good cop in this drama.

The caviar was a nice touch. I had to hand it to him.

I had never tried caviar before. Didn't know the first thing about how to do it correctly. I knew from what I'd read that people eat it with those little pancakes, called blinis. But how? My inclination would be to spoon some caviar onto a blini, roll it up, and eat it like a burrito. But I was guessing that wasn't correct.

Gordon and Kilcullen were probably counting on the fact that I wouldn't know what to do, and they were using this gambit to throw me off my game, to remind me who held all the power in this scenario.

The problem was, it was working.

I could have made any number of wisecracks in response to Kilcullen's invitation. If I wanted to put on my reporter's hat, I could have asked what the taxpayers of New Hampshire would have thought if they knew what Gordon was having for breakfast that day. If I wanted to be flip, I could have said the caviar wasn't the only fishy thing in that room.

"No thanks, I'm fine," was all I managed to say.

"You see, here's the thing," Gordon said, leaning toward me in his chair. "We have a very important election coming up this fall, and your unfounded suspicions could be troublesome to our campaign efforts. We can't afford to have this kind of negative publicity."

He took a copy of the *Herald* from his desk and held it up. Not surprisingly, Sam's story was featured prominently on the front page above the fold of the print edition.

"Well, if what you say is true," I said, "then I don't think you have anything to worry about. I only go where the evidence takes me."

"So you'll forget about this witch hunt, and we can all move on?"

"I didn't say that. I just said I would follow the evidence—*wherever* it might lead."

Gordon's face grew red, and the muscles in his face twitched.

"We've answered your questions, Hanson. I think we've been more than accommodating. And so far, neither you nor the police have produced *any* evidence connecting this administration with the alleged crimes of my former college associate."

I endured the full force of his fiery gaze. It was all I could do not to look away.

"I think you're forgetting who you're dealing with," he added, rising from his chair. "I can squash you like a bug, you *pathetic son of a bitch*."

Gordon's words should have frightened me, but for some reason, they had the opposite effect. Something inside me clicked, and I no longer felt nervous staring him down.

Gordon had made a key tactical error. As long as the threat of his power remained implied, lurking in the shadows like the killer in a slasher film, he was firmly in control. But as soon as the implied threat was made explicit, my fight-or-flight response kicked in.

I might not be the most self-assured or physically imposing person—thank God it's said the pen is mightier than the sword—but I'm stubborn as hell and I don't back down easily.

Maybe it's pride, or maybe it's just stupidity. But if you come at me head on, I'm going to dig in my heels.

"I suppose you can be forgiven for not knowing who *you're* dealing with," I said, standing up as well. "After all, you've got a whole state to run and a criminal conspiracy to cover up. In the words of Prince Humperdinck from *The Princess Bride*, you're swamped. But if you think you can threaten me and I'll just back off, you're sorely mistaken. Next time, make sure you have your errand boy do his homework more thoroughly."

Gordon's face was now a bright shade of scarlet. But there was something glinting in his eyes as well.

Was it fear? The rage of someone who's been entitled his whole life and was finally being challenged for the first time? Or simply an acknowledgment of guilt, a look that suggests: "I know you know?"

I headed for the door, but paused before leaving the room.

"And by the way, you were wrong when you called my suspicion a 'theory' before. It was only a hypothesis. But after seeing how desperate you are to chase me off your trail, you'd better believe it's a theory now. I'm more convinced than ever of your guilt—and you can be damned sure I'm going to prove it."

* * *

My adrenaline was pumping as I practically skipped down the State House steps. I thought I knew what Big Papi must have felt like when he hit that grand slam into the Red Sox bullpen

201

to tie the game in the bottom of the eighth inning during the 2013 playoffs against the Tigers.

I got into my car, started it up, and looked in the rear view mirror.

When I saw a pair of cold, gray eyes staring back at me, I jumped so high I nearly hit my forehead on the windshield.

"If you enjoy your life and want to hold onto it a little longer, you'll do exactly as I say."

I didn't recognize the man who spoke those words. But I recognized his gun. It had a silencer attached to the end of the barrel.

I was looking at the other assailant who'd tried to kill me in my apartment a few weeks earlier.

My heart sank into my stomach as I realized I was so amped up from the clash with Gordon that I'd let my guard down, and I had failed to notice the thug in the back seat of my car.

That mistake could cost me dearly.

The guy in the back seat told me to turn left onto North Main Street and head for Route 3 north. I thought about deliberately crashing the car, but I quickly rejected the idea. There was no way I could guarantee that other people wouldn't be hurt in the accident.

My best bet, I thought, was to let this current hand play out while looking for another opportunity to escape.

As we approached Blossom Hill Cemetery on the left, the goon in the back seat told me to turn into the cemetery. As soon as we were shielded from the road by a clump of trees, he had me pull the car over.

I felt a small, claw-like hand wrap around my face, and the smell of chloroform made me choke. Then everything went dark.

Chapter 22

When I came to, I was lying on my back in the middle of a forest clearing.

A strong breeze gave me a slight chill. The sun was still shining brightly, but it was halfway on its trek toward the horizon. I figured it was around four o'clock in the afternoon.

There was no sign of the creep who'd ambushed me. However, sitting in a weathered Adirondack chair in front of a hunting cabin near the edge of the clearing was Hammond. He was dressed in camouflage fatigues and had a rifle on his lap. A large Bowie knife was sheathed on his belt, and a black-and-tan bloodhound lay curled at his feet.

"How are you feeling?" Hammond said as I sat up and rubbed my head. "No worse for the wear, I hope?"

My head felt foggy and my extremities felt heavy, like my arms and legs were pillowcases filled with wet sand.

"I'm swell, thanks for asking. Can I get a hot towel and a glass of your best cabernet? Just put it on my tab."

"How about some water instead?" Hammond stood up and approached me with a canteen in his hand. "Drink up—you'll need your strength."

I hesitated for a second before taking the flask he offered.

But then my thirst got the better of me. Besides, I figured Hammond wouldn't have me drugged and transported up to his hunting cabin just to poison me when I got there.

Snatching the canteen from his hand, I drank four long swallows. "Why did you bring me here?" I asked, bracing for Hammond's response.

A stomach-churning smile splayed across his face.

"When we met before, I talked about hunting and the excitement of the chase. There's nothing like that thrill. I've experienced it while hunting for deer, bears, and wild boar across North America. I've even had it while big game hunting in Africa and while tracking antelope and ibex in Asia. But the problem with excitement is that it loses its appeal at some point. You find yourself constantly having to ramp up the adrenaline to higher and higher levels."

I knew where he was going, and I thought I might be ill.

"The one thing I haven't tried before is hunting a human being."

"You're a sick fuck," I spat.

He laughed. "Actually, I could kill you now, but what I have in mind is more sporting. At least this way you'll have a slim chance of survival."

Lucky me.

The wind had picked up, and its encircling grasp felt cold against the thin layer of sweat covering my skin.

"What are the rules of this 'game' you're proposing?" I managed to say.

A gleam of excitement flashed in his eyes as he relished the thought.

"This cabin sits deep in the woods and is reachable only by a network of old logging trails. There's no cellular service, and the nearest road is at least ten miles away. On my signal, you'll have a five-minute head start to travel on foot in any direction. Someone who's in decent shape should be able to travel at least a quarter of a mile in that time, maybe even half a mile. When the five minutes are up, the hunt is on."

Pointing to the dog at the end of the leash he was holding, he said, "This is Minerva. She's a purebred bloodhound."

Minerva. So that's where the name "Minerva Enterprises" came from.

"I've trained her as a hunting dog since she was just a pup," Hammond continued. "She has nearly three hundred million olfactory receptors and can follow the scent of another animal or human even if it's several days old. She has the stamina to track for hours and is relentless in the pursuit of her quarry."

"She's beautiful," I said. "How old is she?"

I wanted to keep him talking as long as I could. I was still feeling woozy, and the more time I had to recover, the better my chances were of getting out of there alive.

"She's four years old and weighs over a hundred pounds."

He noticed me eyeing the ATV parked next to the cabin. "If you're thinking about doubling back and taking the ATV, you should know that I hold the only key here in my pocket. And just in case you know how to hotwire a vehicle, I've also drained all the gas. I know where to find more, but if I were you, I wouldn't waste my time looking. By the time you found the extra gas, filled the tank, and managed to start the ATV, we'd have caught up to you for sure."

He took a pair of high-tech goggles from the small waist pack he was carrying. "These are night vision goggles. They allow us to extend our little game past dark. If Minerva and I haven't found you by midnight tonight, I'll call off the search.

If you can survive until then, you're free to go—assuming you can find your way out of these woods alive, that is. And to make it even more sporting, I'm going to let you keep that knife you have in your pocket."

After losing my all-purpose knife to the New Hampshire state trooper a few weeks earlier, I had purchased a new one. "A Swiss Army knife against a rifle, a Bowie knife, a bloodhound, and night vision goggles? Yeah, that seems real sporting of you."

He ignored my remark and tapped a button on his watch. "Your five minutes begins now. I suggest you run."

***

There were three obvious trails leading from the clearing. I thought about taking the trail that disappeared into the woods next to the cabin, but if Hammond was telling the truth about the cabin being ten miles from the nearest road, then I doubted I could remain ahead of him by staying on the trails the whole time. That would just make it simple for Hammond to track me.

Only six months removed from heart surgery, I was pretty sure I didn't have the stamina to win a foot race.

Instead, I chose a trail headed downwind from the clearing. I had no illusions that it would be easy to shake a pursuing bloodhound, but if I had any chance at all, keeping downwind might give me the best shot.

I hurried up the trail at a jogging pace. I wanted to put as much distance between Hammond and me as I could, but I didn't want to expend all my energy out of the gate.

About a quarter of a mile into the woods, the trail became

rockier as it started climbing. As I clambered up the trail, I was keenly aware of how poorly dressed I was for what seemed like a batshit-crazy episode of *Survivor*.

In preparation for my meeting with the governor that morning, I was wearing a maroon polo shirt, gray dress pants, and black leather Oxford dress shoes that hadn't been broken in yet. The new shoes pinched my feet as I slid and scrambled over the rocks, lacking any sort of traction that would aid in my escape.

After a few minutes of climbing, I ducked into the underbrush on the side of the trail, looking for cover. I took out my phone and checked for a signal, but Hammond had been correct: We were too remote.

As if to confirm that Hammond was now on my trail, I heard the faraway sound of Minerva's loud baying as she picked up on my scent. Remembering the strategy that had saved me from the two thugs who broke into my apartment in the middle of the night, I thought about how I might create a set of diversions.

Fooling a bloodhound was going to be a lot tougher than fooling a person, however.

I started by trying to muddle my tracks. I headed into the woods for about a hundred yards, then picked out a large tree that could serve as a landmark.

I veered to my left and looped around the tree in a series of ever-widening clockwise spirals. After three or four loops, I continued on into the forest at an angle from the direction I was originally heading.

I didn't suspect I would throw Minerva off my tracks completely. But I was hoping I might confuse her enough to widen the gap between Hammond and me.

I repeated this practice every few hundred yards or so, finishing each time by setting off in a slightly different direction than I was traveling before—but all the while continuing generally downwind.

After twenty minutes in the forest, I was exhausted. My pace had slowed to little more than a rapid lurch. My sides hurt, and my heart was hammering inside my chest. My tongue was stuck to the roof of my mouth, and I wished I had drunk more of the water that Hammond had offered.

But I didn't dare stop to rest.

Every few minutes, I would hear another deep baying sound as the dog picked up on my trail again. Her cries were no farther away than when I first heard them. If anything, they were getting closer.

I realized I wasn't going to lose Hammond in the forest. In fact, the deeper into the woods I traveled, the slimmer my chances became. So, I changed course by ninety degrees in an attempt to reconnect with the trail.

I couldn't outrun Hammond, and with his bloodhound tracking my scent, I wasn't going to evade him, either. It occurred to me that if I was going to survive, I would have to confront him face to face.

Because Hammond had a rifle, the confrontation would have to take place at close range. Somehow, I'd have to conceal myself well enough that he wouldn't see me until I was upon him.

But the existence of Minerva made that problematic.

Hammond's cabin provided the perfect cover for an ambush. Even if Minerva tipped him off that I was hiding inside, Hammond would be vulnerable as he entered the enclosure. Assuming I could make it back to the cabin before he caught up with me, I might have a fighting chance.

But that was a big ask. My legs felt like linguini and my feet like blocks of granite. I wasn't so sure that my heart wouldn't just give out soon.

Could I reach the cabin before Hammond had me in his sights?

I saw a glimmer of sunlight up ahead where the trees thinned, and I quickened my pace. Stumbling out onto the trail, I hurried down the slope as quickly as my fatigued state allowed.

* * *

As the clearing with Hammond's cabin came into view, I broke into a sprint.

The sound of Minerva's baying pierced the silence. Though I had no way of knowing for sure, it sounded like she and Hammond were only a few hundred yards behind.

When I reached the clearing, I considered skirting its circumference to reach the cabin so I wouldn't be as exposed. But I feared that would take too long. Instead, I dashed straight across to the cabin on the other side.

I reached the door, turned the handle, and pushed.

Locked.

Kneeling down to pick the lock, I felt incredibly vulnerable. The sound of baying grew louder and louder, but I couldn't risk breaking my concentration to look back.

With every second that passed, I braced for the impact of a bullet in my spine.

After what seemed like an eternity, I felt the lock's tumblers fall into place—and I threw open the door.

Wham!

As I hurled myself through the doorway, the wood in the door frame next to me exploded. A split second later, I heard the sharp crack of Hammond's rifle.

I shut the door behind me. The door wouldn't latch because of the damage to the frame, but that didn't matter. I wasn't planning to barricade myself inside; I just wanted enough shelter to engage Hammond without being shot at first.

If Hammond had taken that shot when he first saw me, then I had maybe thirty or forty seconds before he would reach the cabin. I looked around the structure, cursing under my breath as my eyes took a few moments to adjust to the dimness.

It looked like the cabin provided no running water or electricity, just a place for shelter.

The inside was one large room, with a fireplace opposite the door. Next to the wall on the right-hand side was a table and two folding metal chairs. A kerosene lantern sat on the table. Against the wall on the left was a futon with a pillow.

I took off my shirt, stuffed it with the pillow, and placed it on the futon. I was hoping that if Hammond let the dog into the cabin first, she might be distracted enough by my scent on the pillow not to reveal my true position right away.

Then, I grabbed the table and placed it next to the edge of the doorway opposite the side with the hinges. I stood on the table to elevate my torso above the height that Hammond would be expecting.

Spying a wooden broomstick propped against the cabin wall near the door, I was seized with a sudden inspiration. I grabbed the broomstick, and with the few remaining seconds I had before Hammond came through the door, I used my knife to whittle the end to a sharp point.

As I was doing this, I heard Hammond outside the cabin

door.

"You've just made yourself a sitting target. Do you realize that?"

I remained silent, my eyes fixed on the door.

The cabin door slowly creaked open. The bloodhound entered the room first, sniffing around until she spotted me standing on the table—at which point she began to bay powerfully.

I wasn't paying attention to the dog. I was watching the doorway intently as the barrel of Hammond's rifle inched forward.

Suddenly it swung toward me, before Hammond had even entered the room.

Luckily I was prepared, and I managed to react quickly. Lunging forward, I grasped the barrel with my left hand and pushed it toward the ceiling as Hammond fired.

The momentum of my move pulled Hammond into the cabin, and with my right arm I drove the point of the broomstick toward his neck. I missed my mark, and the makeshift spear plunged into his left shoulder just below the collarbone.

Hammond screamed in pain and dropped the rifle. A crazed look appeared in his eyes as he unsheathed the Bowie knife with his right hand.

The ten-inch blade gleamed in the dim light of the cabin as Hammond raised the knife, and I felt a shudder creep over my body. With the blood-thinning medication I was taking after my surgery, even a minor gash could cause me to bleed out quickly.

Fortunately, I was still holding the broomstick in my right hand.

Using the entire weight of my body, I launched myself off the table and pushed Hammond backwards with the broomstick. His head smacked against the stone fireplace and he dropped the knife, slumping to the floor.

I pulled the spear out of his shoulder, and blood spurted from the wound.

I stood over him, watching as his breathing became more labored. Neither of us said a word as we looked at each other. There was nothing more to say.

After a minute or two, he lay still.

Sensing the death of her master, the bloodhound let out a mournful howl.

*　*　*

I was safe from Hammond. But I still needed to get out of the woods alive.

In Hammond's waist pack, I found a map of the forest, a compass, a GPS device, and a waterproof container of matches. In his pants pocket, I found the key to the ATV and what appeared to be a burner phone.

I lit the kerosene lantern and took a closer look around the cabin. In doing so, I noticed the outline of a trap door in the floor.

Opening the door, I discovered that it led to a crawl space containing five-gallon jugs of fresh water and gasoline, as well as more kerosene for the lantern, a few folded plastic tarps, a large spool of twine, an ax, a shovel, and a cooler with what looked to be deer meat preserved among large chunks of ice.

By that time, it was nearly seven o'clock. Too late in the evening to navigate the forest trails before dark.

I went outside, chopped up some wood from the forest, and

started a fire in the pit next to the Adirondack chair. To my surprise, Minerva joined me outside and lay at my feet.

I thought she might see me as a threat for killing her master, but instead she leaned into my touch as I pet her.

Perhaps in some instinctive way she understood that I was just fighting for my survival. Or maybe she was just lonely and in need of affection.

Next to the fire pit stood a small folding table with some cooking utensils, a mess kit, a kettle, a plastic tub for washing, and a metal grate for the fire.

I let the fire get hot, and then I cooked two venison steaks on the grate: one for me and one for Minerva. I filled a bowl of water for the dog and gulped down almost an entire canteen of water myself.

I had no intention of sleeping in the cabin while Hammond's body was there. So, after I'd eaten dinner, I fashioned an outdoor shelter from some sticks and one of the tarps from the crawlspace. I brought the blanket from the futon outside and placed it under the shelter.

I sat by the fire with Minerva for a long time, just stroking the dog and staring into the flames.

It was almost eleven o'clock when I finally stopped placing logs onto the embers. After the fire had burned out, I poured water over the coals and crawled under the tarp to sleep.

When Minerva joined me under the tarp and rested her head on my stomach, I realized she had formed a deep bond with me. Truth be told, I felt the same way about her.

I was going to have to get used to no longer living alone.

Being chased through the woods by a lunatic with a gun had been traumatic, and I had no idea how this madness would affect me in the future. But now that the danger had passed, I felt strangely grateful for what had transpired for two reasons.

I had found a new companion.

And with Hammond's burner phone in my possession, I finally had a way to link Gordon with his crimes.

Chapter 23

Three nights later, I was sitting in the front seat of an unmarked police car with Detective Connor. We were in the parking lot of the Holiday Inn in Tilton, and he was tipping a grape-flavored Pixy Stix into his mouth.

"Gotta lay off the powder," I told him. "That stuff will kill you."

"Ha, ha," Connor replied. "Don't quit your day job."

"Day job? It's 11:30 p.m."

Although I seemed outwardly relaxed, my emotions were a Class Five rapids under the surface. If all went according to plan, we would be taking down Gordon in less than an hour.

* * *

When I woke up outside Hammond's cabin Tuesday morning, I made a fire and cooked another venison steak for Minerva. As soon as she'd had food and water, I gassed up the ATV and secured the cabin door as best I could. With Minerva perched on the seat beside me, we navigated our way out of the woods.

Once I had a cell phone signal, I called Connor. He and Detective Bernardi met me at a gas station on Route 2, and I led them to Hammond's cabin.

"Jesus, Hanson," Bernardi said as he surveyed the blood-soaked scene. "You survived quite a tussle."

Normally, Connor and his partner would have brought in the state police to question me and process the crime scene. But when I explained the opportunity we had to catch Gordon and what I was thinking, they agreed to break with protocol in this case.

My plan required Gordon to believe that Hammond was still alive. If we brought in the staties, they would have to keep Hammond's death under wraps for a few days, and we weren't sure they would agree to such a request. In fact, we weren't sure we could trust them at all, given the sensitivity of the situation and Gordon's likely involvement.

Connor and Bernardi brought Hammond's burner phone to the Concord police station, while I took an Uber back to Manchester and checked out of my hotel. I figured I was finally safe from Hammond's goons now that their employer was dead. Plus, I didn't think I would be welcome at the hotel with Minerva in tow.

With my new canine companion by my side, I retrieved my Dart from the airport parking lot and returned to my apartment. I introduced Minerva to her new home and gave her a big bowl of water and a ratty old tennis ball to play with. I also called the rental car agency and reported the car stolen. Then, I drove up to Concord to reconnect with Connor and Bernardi.

At the Concord PD, a police lab technician specializing in IT was able to access Hammond's burner phone. The phone turned out to be better than a winning Mega Millions ticket: There were multiple incriminating texts between Hammond and an unfamiliar number identified on the phone as "JG"—which we assumed was Gordon's burner.

The messages implicated both men in the murders of Mark and Maggie, as well as the gun smuggling racket.

"Had 'em all the way," I said.

Connor just rolled his eyes.

At that point, Connor brought in his immediate supervisor, Lieutenant Detective Gary Powers, as well as Chief of Police Colton Drummer. "We can't move forward without a highly coordinated effort," he explained.

Connor and Bernardi briefed the two men on the situation. When Powers heard what we were proposing to do, he was apoplectic.

"What are you, nuts?" he said, the veins in his temples bulging like Schwarzenegger's biceps. "You just left the body of a wanted fugitive in a cabin in the woods in the middle of nowhere, without alerting the state police? Do you know how many rules you've broken? And now you're suggesting we cover up Hammond's death so we can run a sting operation to arrest someone we presume is the *governor of the state?*"

Drummer was more measured in his response.

"Frank, I understand what you're looking to accomplish here. I really do. But this isn't something we should be handling by ourselves."

"This isn't something we should be handling, *period,*" Powers said. "We can't just arrest the governor like he's some common criminal."

"Lieutenant, you read those texts," Connor said. "If the governor sent them, he deserves to be held accountable. No one should be above the law." Turning to Drummer, he said, "I get what you're saying, Chief. But we don't know who we can trust, and we can't afford a leak in an operation this delicate. I don't think we can afford to bring the state police into this."

"You're probably not going to like this suggestion," I said. "But what if we call in Agent Gilmartin from the ATF to help us run point? I know you'd prefer not to work with the feds on this, but it's better than taking it to the staties."

Powers looked like I'd run over his dog with my car.

"Why the fuck are we listening to *you*?" he said, pointing to me. "You don't even carry a weapon. I heard your lady friend had to save your ass up in Pittsburg last week."

"You know, courage can take many forms," Connor replied, addressing his supervisor. "You don't need to carry a gun to be brave."

I nodded my appreciation.

"Gentlemen, let's all calm down," Drummer said. "What Parker is suggesting makes sense. Frank, why don't you call Agent Gilmartin, and we'll set up a meeting to discuss the operation."

* * *

Later that night, I was back at the Concord police station, sitting in a conference room with Connor, Bernardi, Drummer, Powers, Agent Gilmartin, and two other ATF agents.

"Agents Gilmartin, Mendoza, Shannon," the chief said, gesturing to our visitors from the federal government, "it's nice to have you aboard."

"So, what have you got?" Gilmartin said, skipping over the pleasantries.

Drummer quickly brought the agents up to speed. For a fleeting moment, Gilmartin looked impressed that I'd been able to overpower Hammond. But then her face resumed its normal stoic look.

"Hammond's death and the discovery of his burner phone have presented us with a key opportunity to capture his co-conspirator, whom we believe to be New Hampshire Governor Jack Gordon," Drummer said.

The ATF agents exchanged surprised glances.

Drummer showed the agents a string of incriminating texts between Hammond and the person identified only as "JG" on Hammond's phone.

"We plan to lure Gordon to a meeting using Hammond's burner phone," he said. "If he shows up to the meeting, this will obviously confirm his identity as Hammond's co-conspirator and implicate him in Hammond's crimes. However, our plan will only work if he believes Hammond is still alive. Given the sensitive nature of our operation, we were hesitant to involve the state police, as we couldn't risk any leaks to the governor's office. Agent Gilmartin, can you send a team to Hammond's cabin upstate to retrieve his body and process the scene? Hanson has a map that can help your agents find it."

Gilmartin nodded to Mendoza, who left the room to make the required phone calls.

"So, we need to craft a message to Gordon from Hammond's burner phone that will convince him to want to meet in person?" Gilmartin said.

"Yes, exactly."

We spent the next twenty minutes debating what the message should say. Eventually, we sent a text to "JG" from Hammond's burner phone, resulting in the following exchange:

[Hammond] *I got Hanson. He's no longer a problem.*
[JG] (Thumbs up emoji)

[Hammond] *Before he died, he told me about some intel the Herald reporter had that could be bad for you. We need to talk.*

[JG] *So call me.*

[Hammond] *Not on the phone. Holiday Inn Tilton, midnight Thu. Rm 110.*

[JG] *Ok.*

We chose Thursday night because we wanted to give Gordon enough notice to clear his schedule if necessary. Plus, the extra time would help us prepare and coordinate the arrest with the Tilton police.

We put a lot of thought into the location for the sting operation. After considering all the motels off of Route 93 between Concord and Lincoln, we chose the Holiday Inn in Tilton because Chief Drummer was friendly with the chief of police in Tilton. We figured their personal relationship might keep the Tilton police chief from asking too many questions about the nature of the operation, as we wanted to limit the number of people who knew who the target was.

The trap finally set, all I had to do was stay out of sight for another forty-eight hours to make sure Gordon believed I was dead.

With the sorry state of my social life, that was easy enough to accomplish.

* * *

"You're looking pretty good for a guy who's supposed to be dead," Connor said as we waited outside the Tilton motel for Gordon to show.

"My undertaker is a creative genius."

The clock on the dashboard of Connor's car read 11:40. As slowly as those digits were advancing, I was sure the clock was malfunctioning.

"By the way, I've got an update on the investigation into Hammond's businesses," Connor added. "The ATF subpoenaed all records related to his restaurants and his car dealership, as well as his forestry company. Not only was he smuggling guns into Canada, but there's evidence to suggest he was laundering money through his other businesses."

"Well, there goes his Citizen of the Year award."

Connor's two-way radio crackled. "Breaker one-nine, this here is Buford T. Justice," Bernardi drawled. "What's the ETA on the Bandit?"

Connor picked up his radio and pressed the talk button. "Those movies came out before you were born," he said. "How do you even know that reference?"

"I was a latchkey kid. My mom worked two jobs when I was growing up. I would come home from school and watch hours of cable television."

"Explains a lot," Connor said.

Detective Bernardi was stationed in Room 110 with Agent Gilmartin. There were two other unmarked cars in the parking lot with us. One of them held ATF agents Mendoza and Shannon, and the other contained two plainclothes officers from Tilton.

Normally, Gordon would be traveling with a state police detail. For this covert meeting, he would most likely be alone. However, we couldn't just assume that.

Our plan was for Mendoza and Shannon to cover Gordon's car in case he had a state trooper escort. Connor would approach Gordon from the rear as Bernardi and Gilmartin surprised him from the hotel room. The two Tilton officers would provide backup in case things went south.

Connor's radio went silent again, and I shifted in the passenger's seat of his car. I could swear I heard a clock ticking somewhere, even though the timepiece on the dashboard display was digital.

11:42.

"You must have some good stakeout stories," I said to break the silence. "What's your best one?"

Connor thought for a few seconds.

"I was watching the front entrance to the Hotel Concord a few years ago. Guy in a tux shirt and bow tie crosses the street and approaches our car. He's carrying a to-go bag with two giant ribeye steaks, and he hands them to us through the car window. Room service, courtesy of the guy we were watching for."

"No kidding, that actually happened to you?"

"Yup. This was before Marco had joined the force. My partner at the time was going through a divorce, had eaten mostly frozen TV dinners for like a month straight. I told him we weren't eating the food, we needed to concentrate on our job. Maybe the dinners were intended to tweak us, but just as likely they were meant to distract us while our subject slipped out. My partner goes, 'I don't care if we lose him or not. I've been eating shit for weeks. This is the best fuckin' steak I've ever had.'"

I laughed. "I was on a stakeout in Beverly Hills once, and the guy gave me the slip by sticking a banana in my car's tailpipe."

"Jesus, do you ever stop?"

"Sorry. When I'm all wound up, my natural defense is to

make jokes. Actually, my best stakeout story is from when I'd just gotten my PI license. I was watching a guy who was wearing a red baseball cap. This was back before half the people in New Hampshire were wearing them.

"Anyway, he's at the Cheshire Fair and I'm watching him at the request of his wife, who's visiting her mother in South Carolina. The wife thinks he might be cheating while she's gone. After I've been following him around for about an hour, he goes into the tractor pull, but that event requires a separate ticket that I hadn't purchased. So, I wait outside the tractor pull for him to come back out.

"As people are leaving the tractor pull, I'm ignoring all the men without hats and concentrating solely on the others. Finally I spot my guy with the red hat and resume my tail. He waits in line for some fried dough, but leaves the window with four pieces in his hands. A woman approaches him with two young kids tagging along behind her. He hands out the fried dough to everyone, and the kids are climbing all over him like he's their father. I'm thinking, *He isn't just cheating, he's got another whole family on the side.*"

"Lemme guess. You picked up the wrong guy coming out of the tractor pull."

"You got it. I was so focused on the red hat that I didn't even notice."

"Details matter."

As the clock changed to 11:53, the flash of headlights illuminated the parking lot, and we ducked down in our seats. A dark blue Lexus cruised through the parking lot and eased into a space in front of the motel.

A surge of excitement coursed through my entire body.

Connor picked up his radio and whispered: "Marco, we have

eyes on the target. Be ready."

The driver emerged from the Lexus wearing a plain gray hooded sweatshirt, blue sweatpants, and cross trainers that looked hardly worn. Not exactly the governor's usual wardrobe—but perfect for not being recognized.

And besides, Gordon thought he was meeting with an old college pal, not the chairman of the state senate.

"Remember," Agent Gilmartin murmured over the radio. "Everyone moves in as soon as we open the door."

"Copy that," Connor said.

The hood of his sweatshirt casting a dark shadow over his face, Gordon approached the door to Room 110 and knocked sharply three times. After a few beats, the door flew open to reveal Gilmartin and Bernardi pointing their pistols at Gordon's chest.

At the same time, Connor threw open the car door and sprinted up behind Gordon with his service revolver drawn, and I saw Mendoza and Shannon spring into action and cover the Lexus.

I remained in the front seat of Connor's car, watching the drama unfold.

"On your knees and get your hands in the air, *now!*" Gilmartin barked.

Gordon put up his hands and slowly dropped to his knees as Gilmartin ordered. Connor cuffed Gordon's hands behind his back and pulled down the hood obscuring his face.

Shock and disappointment battled for control of my emotions as I realized the person kneeling in front of the hotel room door wasn't Gordon after all.

It was Kilcullen.

Chapter 24

Ninety minutes later, I was sitting on the other side of a one-way mirror, watching an exasperated Connor interview Kilcullen in an interrogation room at the Concord police station.

"So you're telling me it was actually *you* who was working with Hammond this whole time, and Governor Gordon knew nothing about it?"

"Yes, that's right."

"You claim this is your phone," Connor said, holding up the burner he took from Kilcullen during the booking process, "and that *you* were the one who sent all these messages to Hammond?"

"Again, that's correct."

"How do you explain the fact that Hammond referred to you as 'JG' on his phone?"

"I have no idea. You'll have to ask him. Maybe it's short for Judy Garland, because he knows my dog's name is Toto. Maybe 'BK' was already taken because he has Burger King on his speed dial."

I couldn't stand to watch Kilcullen lie for another second, so I got up and took a walk outside.

When I returned to the station, it was after two in the

morning. Kilcullen was in a holding cell, and Connor was back at his desk filing a report.

"Get anything useful?" I asked.

"Nope. Kilcullen is sticking by his story. Says he met Hammond at a state function, and Hammond later offered to pay him good money to rig the government contract in his favor. Kilcullen says the gun smuggling operation was all Hammond's idea and that he was brought into the plan for protection, to keep the staties and other government employees off Hammond's back."

"Whose idea was it to kill Mark and Maggie?"

"Conveniently, Kilcullen said that was all Hammond's idea as well and that he knew nothing about it. He said when he found out that Bowman and Malone had been killed, he thought about going to the police but feared retaliation."

"You're not buying his story, are you?"

"Hell no. I'm with you. Kilcullen is lying to shield his boss."

"What do you think gave us away? Gordon obviously suspected a sting, and he sent Kilcullen to the meeting in his place."

"Maybe it was the tone or the language of our text. Or maybe he was just being cautious. We might never know. The only thing we *do* know is that, even if we're right about Gordon, Kilcullen would do almost anything to protect him."

* * *

I didn't get home until nearly three o'clock in the morning. I took Minerva for a walk, then lay down on my bed without even changing my clothes. I didn't bother setting my alarm, either, as I knew I'd be too tired to go to cardiac rehab in a few hours.

When I woke up later that morning, a light rain was falling. The pale gray sky aptly matched my mood.

Hammond was dead, and his gun smuggling operation was finished. Kilcullen was behind bars, and Boudreau would also be spending a long time in a prison cell for ramming Maggie's car.

As my high school debate coach would say when we scored a cheap victory because the other team had to forfeit: "Take the win."

Yet, all I could think about was Gordon sitting smugly in the governor's mansion, untouched. And the more I thought about it, the angrier I got.

I couldn't understand what would motivate Kilcullen to cover for him. What unholy influence did Gordon hold over Kilcullen—and why?

Did Gordon have highly embarrassing photographs or other compromising information on Kilcullen? If so, it would have to be pretty explosive material for Bryce to take the fall for Gordon's crimes.

Maybe it was simply the allure of money, although Kilcullen wouldn't be spending any of it for a long, long time.

I had to see for myself what Kilcullen was thinking. So, I called the Concord police department and arranged to visit him in jail.

I wanted Kilcullen to look me in the eye and tell me why he was lying. Maybe I could even convince him to come clean about Gordon's involvement.

Sure, it was a long shot. But I couldn't stomach the idea of Gordon walking away scot-free.

The New Hampshire Attorney General's office and the ATF

were arguing over who would get to try Kilcullen in what order. The state wanted its accessory-to-murder charges to take priority over the federal gun smuggling crimes, but the ATF was pulling rank as a federal agency.

While they were sorting all this out, Kilcullen was in jurisdictional limbo. He was sitting in a holding cell in Concord until the state and the feds could reach an agreement.

By the time I secured the necessary clearance to see him, it was late in the afternoon. The holding area of the Concord jail smelled of stale sweat and urine.

Kilcullen was in a cell by himself, sitting with his back against the wall. He wore a gray jumpsuit. His legs were stretched out in front of him, his feet crossed at the ankles. He was reading a book on investing.

"Expecting a windfall soon?" I said, pointing to the book. "Maybe a nice fat payoff for taking the rap for your boss?"

He looked at me as if I were a mild curiosity. Like a strange bug he'd discovered when picking up a rock.

"I don't know what you're talking about."

"Come on, nobody's fooling each other here. I know what you did, and you know that I know. I'm just trying to understand *why*."

He set the book down and crossed his arms defiantly. "We're not doing this."

I sighed, then gently rapped on the bars of his cell with my knuckles.

"You're an Ivy League graduate, Bryce. Probably used to wearing Italian silk shirts, sipping single malt scotch, eating lobster and caviar, smoking a fine Cuban after dinner. You're really willing to give all that up for the next twenty years for a slimeball like Gordon, who'd sell you out to save himself in a heartbeat?"

No response.

"You know, if you're scared of Gordon, I'm sure the feds have already told you they can protect you and your family."

"Scared?" That got a rise out of him. "You're so far off base."

"Okay, then steer me in the right direction. What has Gordon ever done for you?"

Kilcullen got up and approached the bars of his cell. He was so close that I could see the pores in his oily skin.

"Do you have any children, Hanson?"

"No."

"I have two kids. A twelve-year-old daughter and an eight-year-old son. Can you imagine the concern that a parent must feel when his youngest child, who was seven at the time, comes to him and says it feels like somebody's knocking on his skull from the inside?"

I'm not always very bright. But I knew enough to be quiet and let Kilcullen finish.

"And can you imagine the anguish you feel when you take your child to the doctor and he informs you that your son has cancer? You'll do anything to make sure your child lives to see his next birthday, and then the next one. You would give your life to make sure he can grow up and have a life of his own. Get his license, have his first kiss. Graduate from high school. Drink his first beer. Get a job. Start a family. All the things we take for granted every day."

He dropped his voice to barely a whisper.

"If you're lucky enough to be in a position of means, then you take your kid to the best oncologists at one of the top hospitals in the country. And when you hear there's a new experimental drug that looks promising in trials, but it's not covered by insurance and it costs five thousand dollars per dose, then what do you do? Tell me, Parker: If you were a parent, what would *you* do?"

I wanted to tell him that thousands of families are in the same position every year, but they don't participate in a criminal conspiracy that involves the illegal sale of firearms across an international border. They don't cover up the murders of multiple people or shield powerful leaders from prosecution just so they can afford a medical treatment.

I wanted to remind him that he was the chief advisor for the governor of a US state, someone with the power to enact a practical solution to the very real lack of access to vital health care that millions of Americans face every day.

But those remarks wouldn't make any difference. I realized there was nothing I could say that would convince Kilcullen to give up Gordon. And seeing the pain in Kilcullen's eyes, I figured it wasn't the time for a lecture, either. I even felt a little sympathy for him.

"I'm sorry to hear about your son," I replied. "I hope he makes a full recovery."

And with that, I left the holding area.

* * *

I stopped by the Tipsy Moose on my way home from the jail. Amalia was working behind the bar. But she was busy and didn't see me right away.

I sat on a stool at the far end of the bar and gazed absently at the TV screens scattered around the room. The Sox were playing the Orioles on some of the screens. No score in the bottom of the second.

It's been said that baseball can teach us an important lesson in failure.

The highest career on-base percentage in the majors, .482, belongs to former Red Sox legend Ted Williams. Babe Ruth is next, at .474.

According to conventional wisdom, if even these all-time greats failed to reach base safely in more than half their plate appearances, then we mere mortals shouldn't feel bad about our own futility.

That notion gave me little comfort, though. And as I tapped my fingers rhythmically against the bar, I realized why.

Baseball isn't an accurate metaphor for life.

In baseball, it doesn't matter who you are or where you come from: The distance between home plate and first base is ninety feet for every batter. Whether the sun is shining overhead or heavy rains have turned the base paths into a quagmire, both teams play on the same field and in the same conditions.

In baseball, there is order and symmetry and beauty. The struggle takes place between neatly chalked lines, and talent is all that matters for success.

The same can't be said about life.

Knowing that Gordon was going to get away with everything would have stung regardless. But it would have been much easier to accept if it had at least been a fair fight. The fact that his money and power made him untouchable—and there was *nothing* I could do about it—was like pouring gasoline into an open wound.

No, I thought as I surveyed the bar from my stool. Baseball isn't a metaphor for life. It's a respite *from* life, from the ugliness and the injustice and the pain.

Life is what happens *after* the game. It's the mess of empty peanut shells and candy wrappers strewn all over the stadium. It's the chaos in the tunnels as everyone rushes for the exits. It's the snarl of traffic as thousands of people leave the stadium at once, the honking of horns and the indiscriminate flashing of middle digits as drivers look out only for themselves.

Maybe that's why we like sports so much. For a few hours at a time, we can lose ourselves in an artificial environment that gives us the illusion of fairness. There is unpredictability in sports, but it's contained within a tidy world of rules that are applied equally, where there's at least the perception that everyone is competing on a level playing field.

And when the game is over, the bubble bursts—and we go back to a reality where con artists prey upon the trusting, the privileged use their power to keep those who are less fortunate oppressed, and people like Gordon add to their considerable fortunes at the expense of others.

It was seven-thirty on the Friday evening before the Fourth of July weekend, and the bar was filling quickly. As I looked out over the crowd, an overpowering sense of weariness consumed me.

How many of these people were taking advantage of someone else, I wondered?

How many had secrets they were keeping from their partners, or schemes they were hiding from the world?

Trying to do the right thing all the time in a world where that feels like the exception, not the rule, is exhausting. It's like walking behind a never-ending ticker tape parade and picking up all the confetti left on the ground—only the parade keeps speeding up and growing larger with every city block.

In that moment, I felt the full weight of that responsibility, and it was crushing.

Just then, Amalia appeared. She gave me a big smile, spun a cardboard coaster down on the bar in front of me, and asked: "Seltzer water and a salad?"

I returned her smile weakly.

"Actually, I'll have a bourbon on the rocks and a bacon cheeseburger. And could you make them both doubles?"

Chapter 25

The next morning was cloudless and cool for early July, the sky resembling an infinite spring-fed lake.

My stomach felt unsettled, which I took as a good sign. It was like my body was reminding me that we had a deal: I would feed it only healthy food from now on, and in return it would keep me alive for at least a few more decades.

I took Minerva for a long walk around my neighborhood. We ended up at Veteran's Memorial Park, where we played fetch with her tennis ball. To my surprise, she could even catch the ball in mid-air, better than some of that season's Red Sox players.

I had a mental image of her playing outfield for the Sox, like in an *Air Bud* movie. *That would give a new twist to the phrase "the dog days of summer,"* I thought.

When we got back to the apartment, I gave Minerva breakfast and made a strawberry-banana smoothie for myself. Checking my messages, I saw that I'd missed three calls the day before while I was visiting Kilcullen in jail.

The first was from Brooke Bowman. She was calling to thank me for everything I'd done, including staying on the case when she'd wanted me to quit.

"Seeing those horrible men get what they deserved," she said, her voice breaking on the phone, "I was finally able to sleep for the first time since Mark's death. And knowing there are fewer guns on the black market today makes me think that maybe he didn't die in vain. I can't begin to tell you how grateful I am."

The second message was from Callie.

"Thank you for checking in on me last week. That was very sweet of you. I wanted to let you know that I'm doing a lot better now, and I'm finally ready for that date any time you're available."

The third message was from someone I'd never met before. He introduced himself as Hector and said he'd read about me in the newspaper.

"I hope you can help me," he said in a thick Spanish accent. "I have a friend whose daughter has gone missing. He is worried about going to the police, because he doesn't want to be deported. We don't know where else to turn."

I called the number that Hector left and told him I would meet with him that morning to discuss his friend's situation. I also called Callie back and made a date with her for later that week: a picnic lunch in Bear Brook State Park in Allenstown.

Then I took a piece of stationery from a drawer in my desk and wrote a note to Brooke:

Dear Brooke,

I'm glad I was able to bring some comfort to you in what is surely a difficult time. But I should be thanking you, not the other way around.

Before I got your message, I was struggling with the idea that I'd somehow failed by not bringing everyone who was involved in your husband's death to justice. Your thoughtful words reminded me that success is measured in many ways.

Mark was a person of incredible bravery and integrity. For these attributes, he and your family have paid the ultimate price. But you're absolutely right: His death did serve a higher purpose. And I'm inspired by his example.

All we can do, all any of us can do, is to be our best selves and hope that's enough.

If you ever need anything, please don't hesitate to ask.
Your friend,
Parker

I sealed the note in an envelope and addressed it to Brooke. I brought the envelope downstairs and placed it with the outgoing mail. Then I returned to my apartment.

I wasn't due to meet with Hector for another hour, so I sat down in front of my laptop. I opened a new browser window and searched for the website of Jack Gordon's main rival in the election that November. I found the campaign's website and clicked on the button at the top marked "Volunteer."

I might not have been able to beat Gordon in a court of law. But I was going to make damned sure he wouldn't win at the polls as well.

Game on.